BELL WITCH:
The Movie NOVEL

BELL WITCH:
The Movie NOVEL

A NOVEL BY

Robert Mickey Maughon M.D.

BASED ON A FILM BY

S. Shane Marr

Bell Witch: The Movie NOVEL by Robert Maughon M.D.
© 2005 by Sugarlands Publishing
All photographs © 2005 Big River Pictures

ISBN 0-976514-10-9

All rights reserved. No part of this book may be reproduced or transmitted in any form or by any means, electronic or mechanical, including photocopying, recording, or by any information storage and retrieval system, without prior written permission of the Publisher, except where permitted by law.

First Edition 2005
1 2 3 4 5 6 7 8 9 10

PROLOGUE

Adams, Tennessee
1932

"I PROMISED MY father, grandfather, and great-grandfather that I would always take care of the family's home and birthplace, Mary Jane. I swore I would never, ever leave." The tall, handsome young man was talking to his infant daughter, who was two weeks old that day.

"I told them this, promised them this, even though I knew what it meant: the demon of a legend that has haunted this family since that cursed year of 1817," he said.

"Mary Jane, every other Bell man has stayed and made it work, even though it has been a horrible struggle. Just about every Bell man . . . but me," Jake grimaced with a disgusted sigh.

The tiny, innocent blonde-haired baby, wrapped snugly in a blanket just a few feet away in her bassinet, was sound asleep and oblivious to her father's fevered discussion that was as much debate as discourse. "But after what has happened to your dear mother, just like the legend said it would. . . . I'm just not going to chance anything else happening to you. We'll be next to impossible to find . . . for anyone or . . . anything where we are going. A new life for me and certainly for you, baby girl." He looked over and managed a faint smile at his baby girl.

Jake Bell grabbed another handful of nails and stuffed them in his Levi's pockets. He bent over and picked up a splintered board and placed it over the last gap of the window he was boarding up.

"But now that your mama's gone, it's just you and me. And we're packing up and leaving. And little Mary Jane, after everything that's happened here—whether this cursed legend had anything to do with your dear mother's death or not—we are leaving!" Jake Bell declared, almost snarling around the nails in his clenched teeth.

He hammered in the final nails. Jake continued to direct his discussion to the baby in the bassinet, but in reality, he knew he was declaring to himself . . . and to the apparition or entity or whoever might be hovering around the land that had been in his family for generations. When the last board was nailed snugly to the window frame, he tossed his hammer and nails to the ground. He rushed over to his baby girl and picked her up out of the bassinet. Jake held her close, tears slowly starting to stream down his face as the emotion overwhelmed him.

"We are leaving this god-forsaken place, Mary Jane, never to return. We are going to build ourselves a new life where no one or no thing will find us," Jake Bell boldly stated, wiping the tears from his face with the back of his wrist, struggling to keep from shouting the words in defiance. With that declaration, the young widower hugged his baby girl as close as he could, wishing he could keep her safe forever.

A solitary black bat circled high and unnoticed directly above them in the clear blue Tennessee sky. Jake Bell pulled himself together, clearing his throat as if to banish a bad taste.

With his daughter on his hip, Jake strode away from the house and land that had been in his family, for better and for worse, for generations.

CHAPTER 1

Adams, Tennessee
1935

A 1928 FORD TRUCK puttered down the dusty one-lane road in Adams, Tennessee, with the tires raising a dust trail that hung in the hot air. It had not rained in Middle Tennessee in a month. The Ford made headway, but barely. No matter, there was no rush to get anywhere fast anyway. Adams, Tennessee, was just a whisper of a town outside Nashville, with absolutely nothing to do there when you did get to where you were going. So why would anyone get in a hurry? As with all Ford trucks of its time, this 1928 model was sturdy, reliable and not flashy. It moved forward, backfired, sputtered and moved ahead a bit more. The Ford truck would get you where you wanted to go, not in a hurry, mind you, but it would get you there. A perfect vehicle for Adams, Tennessee.

This '28 Ford did what you'd expect it to do: sputter, backfire, putter forward . . . and swerve. It swerved down the dusty back road because the two fellas in the vehicle were imbibing the favorite local beverage, whiskey. And the good ol' boy driving shouldn't have been, because he could barely keep it between the ditches.

Which didn't keep him from a running conversation with his buddy, who was looking at him dubiously. "So, for years, some witch tormented this family? What kind of torment? Did she dress up in bed sheets and yell 'Boo!'?"

"Legend has it that she'd whack 'em, slap 'em around—you know, pull their hair, stuff like that," the driver said. "They'd hear her talking to them, a regular female voice. One time early on, she threatened to kill ol' John Bell."

His buddy swore. "Good God, man, give me a break! That's the silliest godawful thing I have ever heard of." The driver shook his head. "Big Boy, I didn't say it was true. It's a legend. I'm just telling you the legend. Legends are based a little bit on fact. Stories throughout history start as legends like this. A bit of fact . . . stretched to the limit." The driver took his hands off the wheel to demonstrate how the truth gets stretched.

"Watch the road!" his fellow drinker yelled; they both grabbed the wheel just in time to keep the truck out of the ditch. An amber Jack Daniel's liquor bottle went rattling across the floorboard. "Like I was saying before I was interrupted, this witch would tell them stuff, like quoting the entire Bible. She was supposed to have the most beautiful singing voice anybody had ever heard."

"You don't say," his partner laughed as he leaned over to grab the nearly empty bottle and take another swig.

"And she would even go to church, for goodness' sakes!" Yanking the bottle from his friend's hand, he continued, "Oh, yeah, and so one day, finally, she just up and killed ol' John Bell." He turned the bottle up and took a final slug.

He said solemnly, "The State of Tennessee recognizes until this day that John Bell was killed by a ghost." Tapping the bottom of the Jack Daniel's bottle to obtain one last drop, he again lost interest in the Ford's steering wheel, almost sending the weaving vehicle into yet another ditch.

He finally caught his inebriated friend's attention with his story—and his driving, or rather, lack thereof. "And you believe all of that, fool?" his buddy laughed.

"I didn't say I believe any of that. That's why we're going there tonight. Like I told you before, even some of Shakespeare's tales are based on an old legend like this one. So who knows?"

"Shakes-who?" comes the drunken response.

"Shakespeare! Oh, forget it. What would you know about literature, anyway? Yes, fool. That's why we're going to the old Bell estate tonight. You see after the Witch, or Haunt, or whatever, that killed old John Bell did the dirty deed, she said she would return in a hundred and seven years. From my calculations, my good friend, that is going to be tonight."

"You mean to say, in your drunken calculations, don't you?"

The driver laughed but didn't deny it.

"How much farther is it? I gotta pee and it's going to get dark in a few hours, so get a move on!"

"Well, I got to urna . . . urni . . . urnm . . . I got to go pee, too. Look, I think it's up the road a bit." He peered uncertainly at the horizon.

"You're lost, fool. Look, there's a farmer up there in front of his house. Let's stop and ask Baldy for directions to wherever it is we're going."

The truck pulled to a creaky stop right in front of a bald-headed old farmer fixing a fence in front of his farmhouse. A woman peeked out from a second-story window.

"Howdy, fellas." The old man stopped from his chores and wiped sweat from his bald pate with a handkerchief he pulled from his back pocket.

"Hi, mister. We're looking for the old Bell farm. You ever heard of it?" The farmer developed a sudden interest in his shoes, didn't say anything.

Undeterred by the silence, the inebriated driver continued, "Word is the witch is coming back this year. We figure it is tonight! We came down from Nashville to see if she will."

The farmer continued to wipe his shiny scalp but didn't say a word.

The drinker said, "Mister, you know where this place is?" The farmer spat tobacco on the ground, splattering juice on the tire of the '28 Ford.

"Bell farm is up the road, boys." He pointed with a small tilt of his head.

"Is ol' John Bell buried close to there? We think that's where she'll visit first."

Tight-lipped, the farmer replied, "Not sure about that, boys."

A heavy-set woman, the farmer's wife, cracked the screen door just enough to get a good view of the foolish visitors.

Before they leave, the driver asked, "You lived in Adams long, old timer?"

"All my life," came the brief reply.

The farmer turned away and walked toward his house. His wife gave the men a hard look, moved away from the door and disappeared into the house. The two Nashville men looked at each other and shrugged. The driver ground the Ford's gears and got underway.

The two men were undeterred, and they pushed forward in the puttering old truck as the evening hues started to color the sky. They drove up the road a ways, watching for the Bell place.

"It's gotta be that road up there."

"Take it, turn in here."

The Ford truck prattled along, heading up the hill. The outline of a house began to appear through the gloom of the trees just ahead. "That's it," the driver shouted as he downshifted and ground the gears again, so instead of backfiring into the yard, they glided to a halt.

"Oh my God, we found it!" the other besotted man observed.

As the truck rattled to a stop, the driver reached down to the floorboard and pulled out an old brick. He dropped heavily off the running board and used the brick to scotch the front tire so the truck wouldn't roll away. He reached in and grabbed the empty Jack Daniel's bottle from the floorboard, hoisting it to his lips as he tried his best to squeeze a little more courage from the amber glass. But alas, there was none.

"Let's go," he said, tossing the bottle into the weeds. In the South, wisteria seemed to be taking over the world. It was swallowing this place, too, covering the front yard and much of the weather-beaten old house. Its shape was an undefined lump under the green mound.

"See, I told you I would get us here," the driver said to his partner as they waded through the vines surrounding the house.

"Now what?"

"Well, let's go inside and see what we can find."

The drunken duo walked all the way up to the boarded-up house and pushed through the thick vines onto the front porch. The two men found a loose board and pulled it aside, trying to peer through the window. Then they went up to the front door and tried the knob. "It's locked."

"Aw, shoot," the driver moaned as he rattled the door knob in disgust. "Now what do we do?" the other asked. His friend went back to the loose board over the window and ripped it off, revealing a still-intact pane of glass. He grabbed a large rock and smashed the window. Now he could squeeze through the hole and over the window sill. He crawled in and disappeared. Before long, he opened the front door from the inside.

"Typical," his partner muttered.

The two breakers-and-enterers walked into the old house.

"Can you believe this place?"

"It kinda gives me the creeps." Unbeknownst to the two drunken revelers, a single black bat began to circle high above the old house in the twilight. Dipping and diving, the bat descended closer to the dilapidated old building.

"Witch . . . hey, Kate. Hey, Kate, you old Bell Witch," the driver brayed. "Come on out. Come out, come out, wherever you are."

Now nervous, his partner in crime said, "Look, this isn't right; I feel like someone is watching us. This ain't our property."

"Yeah, it's Kate," his friend said. "She's the one watching us. I told you she would be back. Kate, can you hear me?" The driver began speaking louder. "Kate, if you can hear me, I'm not afraid of you, come on, old girl, and give me your best shot."

OHHHEEHHOOOHHEE. A slow groan began to emanate from the woodwork. Crack, crack, crack. Flashes of light began to explode from the windows, bursting from the creases and crevices of the house.

"Let's go," the driver shouted, and the two scrambled to get out of the house. They fell down as they blundered through the wisteria, got up and ran as hard as they could from the house that made true believers out of them. They jumped in the truck and slammed the doors shut.

"Come on, come on!" the driver yelled at the Ford. He was shaking all over from fear, and the keys dropped from his trembling hands. He snagged them from the floorboard and stabbed them into the ignition. Over and over the Ford's motor groaned, but it never did fire up completely.

Unable to wait any longer, the rider yelled, "Brother, I am out of here," and scrambled from the truck.

"Wait up," the driver yelled as he too abandoned ship and ran wildly after his friend, taking one last glance at the old vine-covered home.

He was so scared he turned sober, at least for that night.

CHAPTER **2**

Great Smoky Mountains, Tennessee
1943

"TELL US THE story of the Bell Witch. Tell us the story of the Bell Witch," the young voices shouted in unison. Over and over the incessant chant was repeated. Adding to the ceaseless, demanding verbal clamor was the constant rhythmic clapping of four sets of children's hands. Their voices joined perfectly with the coordinated clapping to take the racket to a new level. So much commotion was being created inside the two-story log cabin, nestled in the foothills of the Smoky Mountains, that even the single plume of white smoke emanating from the stone chimney could be seen to dance in the moonlight. The rhythmic clapping and chanting sent the smoke trail in one direction and then another. A smoky white zigzag bizarrely meandered from the chimney, endlessly waltzing right then left, then right again. Upward through the darkened heavens, the drunken plume ascended.

A lone black bat circled the smoke before disappearing above the mountain peaks, a brief shadow obscuring the twinkling stars piercing the sky.

Still and silent at first, a rectangular sheet of snow, loosened by the day's sun, then refrozen after nightfall, was pried loose from the cabin's roof by the vibrations of the pleading, yet increasingly demanding, voices and clapping hands of the youngsters. The ice sheet abruptly slid from the roof and came crashing to the snow-whitened ground outside the log cabin's front door.

"Thump." The noise of the child-induced mini-avalanche accomplished what the repeated, orchestrated coaxing of the gaggle of children could not; it caught the notice of the attractive woman with long raven locks who was caring for them.

"Enough, children, enough!" the exasperated woman exclaimed, seemingly mimicking the children by clapping her long thin hands together to make her point. Finally the boisterous children had done what they had set out to do—they had gotten her attention. She gave them a stern glance as she brushed the soot from her handmade sackcloth dress.

"Please, Miss Katherine, tell us the story of the Bell Witch," seven-year-old Maggie begged. Maggie's short, curly blonde hair dangled over her tilted head, partially hiding her pleading green eyes.

"I'll be in your first grade class next year, and I want to know the story of the Bell Witch that you tell all of your other students." The pixie-like seven-year-old stood with her hands on her hips. "Everyone says you tell the best ghost story of anyone in the mountains," she said. "And Miss Katherine, I want to know the story before I even start the first grade!" Maggie was late starting school at seven, but she had been held out a year because no one could control her. They had hoped she would mature a bit, but she had not. If anything, she was worse.

The school marm, who was in her mid-thirties but looked much younger, stopped stoking the red-coaled fire that crackled, hissed and popped in the massive fireplace. She stood up, steadying herself with a hand on the large limestone mantle covered with dozens of pictures of people, animals, landscapes and old buildings and bridges.

Katherine swept her dark tresses away from her pretty face, seemingly smoothing the furrows from her forehead, put there by her concern with keeping the fire stoked on this cold night. In her attempt to keep the children warm, she had ignored their pleas to tell the most famous ghost story in the State of Tennessee, and one of the most legendary in all of America. Now she could no longer ignore them as they had encircled her and demanded attention. She looked down at the collection of excited youngsters.

Maggie, the youngest at seven, was the daughter of the Reverend and Mrs. Jack Cane. The Reverend preached at the First United Methodist Church in Gatlinburg. He and his wife had two older boys, but Maggie, the baby girl, was their favorite. It showed. Maggie was precocious. She could do no wrong in the eyes of her parents, and young Maggie knew it. The curly-haired little one knew she was going to get her way, as she almost always certainly did—much to the chagrin of most of the parishioners of First United Methodist Church, as little Maggie disrupted services quite regularly.

Maggie's favorite game on Sunday mornings was to wait until her father was midway through the worship service, invariably approaching the most important point aimed at the worst sinners in the congregation. Maggie would then slide out of her front-row pew, eluding the desperate clasping and clutching of her mother. Her new Shirley Temple tap shoes, just recently bought at the Reagan's Store, made loud clacking sounds against the church's just-varnished oak floor. Demonstrating an uncanny ability to tap her shoes in concert with her dad's admonishments to the sinners, Maggie would walk directly to the Reverend Cane's seat next to the pulpit and make herself ostentatiously comfortable. She got only a slight nod from the Reverend acknowledging that she'd be sitting in his seat next to the pulpit until the service was concluded. The tiny Shirley Temple look-alike had learned at an early age that as long as she was the apple of the Reverend Cane's eye, Maggie was going to get her way.

Ten-year-old Andrew was the son of one of the most financially prominent families in town. Jack Reagan and his wife Jane owned the Smoky Mountain Tourist Inn. Wealthy people from around the world had stayed at their hotel while visiting the Smokies. Andrew's family had done well at attracting and keeping many of the tourist's dollars and they were not shy in displaying this ability. Seth was ten years old, the son of the local ne'er-do-well, Johnson Sells. Johnson Sells had been in and out of so many businesses and ventures that people really didn't know how he made his living. Yet the Sells family always seemed to have money, lots of money. The rumor, and probable truth, was that Johnson Sells owned a bootleg liquor business in nearby Cocke County. White lightning—the stuff of legends throughout the Southern Appalachian mountains. In years before, bootleggers had been everywhere in and around Gatlinburg and Sevier County, but now, in 1943, most of the bootlegging had died down close to town. Johnson Sells was a character right out of a morality play. He had been handsome when he was younger, full of charm and plenty smart. He just would rather make a living at something that was not respectable simply because he felt he was smarter than everyone else. His motto was, "Only dummies worked for a living."

Seth Sells had inherited his dad's intelligence, but not his sloth and lack of character. Even though Seth was young, his dad's dark good looks were appearing in him. Seth resented his dad's reputation; it hurt his feelings, if the truth be told. Already, at Seth's tender age, he had declared he wouldn't mess his life up like his dad.

Seth had a reason to try to make his life special. He had already decided what he wanted to do—he wanted to be a country doctor like his hero, Dr. Robert Thomas. Dr. Thomas was the legendary family doctor who covered the surrounding county on horseback, delivering babies, treating snakebites, curing the colic, setting broken legs and treating even the occasional black bear bite. All the families in Sevier County had come to know Dr. Thomas as a hero and local legend. Seth felt he could acquit himself and acquire the same respect of the local folks that Dr. Thomas had if he too could become a physician. Also, even at a young age, Seth had decided he wanted to marry young Mary Jane Bell. It may have been puppy love, but he knew the young girl was the only woman for him and the only way he could escape the pitiful shadow his father cast was to become a man like Dr. Thomas and to marry the most beautiful woman in the mountains, Mary Jane Bell.

Mary Jane was eleven. She was the lone child of craftmaker Jake Bell. With long blonde hair and penetrating blue eyes, even at eleven years old she was poised and womanly. Mary Jane's mother had died in childbirth, so Mary Jane took care of the chores. She was a great help to her father, whose crafts store adjoined their house and his workshop. It would have been impossible for Jake to have kept up his business and his home except for the extraordinary help of his daughter Mary Jane.

Unfortunately for Seth, all of the boys in the area were also in love with Mary Jane. Plus, he was a year younger than her, which at this age, meant she was a lot more mature. Even the boys who were several years older swore they were going to do well in life so they could eventually ask for Mary Jane's hand in marriage. In the mountains, it had always been customary for girls as young as fifteen or even fourteen to get married, so long as the bride and groom had the permission of their parents. No one wanted to admit it, however, but a few shotgun weddings had been performed for brides and grooms of such a tender age. So the boys who pined for Mary Jane knew they wouldn't have to wait too long. Jake and his daughter Mary Jane had moved into Gatlinburg only nine months ago. Not much was known about them except that they had moved from the Nashville area to a small town called Oliver Springs and then to the mountains. Although a quiet man who carefully guarded his privacy, Jake was generally well-liked because he kept up the traditional crafts and was a hard worker. His glasswork was especially good, and wealthy visitors loved to watch Jake create vases, drinking glasses and, of course, bowls, plus exotic objects of different shapes and hues.

"Why in the world Seth, Maggie, Mary Jane and Andrew," Katherine asked, looking at each child as she said their name, "would you children want to hear the legend of some silly ol' witch ghost story from the days of General Andrew Jackson, when we have such a beautifully glorious night?" Katherine swept her raven hair from her face and gestured out the window to the luminous snow-swept landscape backlit with moonlight. Maggie jumped a foot forward at once and began to recite emphatically, tilting her head back and forth like a bobble head doll as she stated her case: "You know this story like no one else. Everyone loves the way you tell the story."

"All right, children, okay," Katherine declared with resignation. "It is true that I know the story of the Bell Witch well. I am from the part of Tennessee where this legend originates." She nodded her head solemnly, letting her young audience know that she would recount the tale, however reluctantly.

Katherine pulled her plain brown dress around her to move it from the heat of the fire. To most this would be a simple gesture, but to the children she was royalty and thus this simple move was viewed as something a movie star would do. "I do tell the story in an entertaining manner," their star acknowledged.

Katherine then pulled a four-pronged chair from beside the now crackling-hot fire and placed it directly in front of her audience. She whisked her long skirt in an elegant fashion to drape around her legs as she sat down. Her young questioners formed a perfect semicircle around Katherine, then simultaneously Andrew, Seth, Maggie and Mary Jane sat on the wooden floor in front of their heroic storyteller.

Andrew and Seth had gently jockeyed to see who would be seated next to Mary Jane. Maggie had not noticed, since she was too young to understand such distractions. Mary Jane had been aware of the manly attention from these two youngsters, but did not care for it. Katherine had seen the seating dilemma and had gently nudged both boys to sit on either side of the pretty young lady so that neither gentleman gained undue advantage. Maggie was so young that she was unaware that Seth and Andrew were ignoring her.

As soon as her audience was settled in and eyes had opened wide in anticipation of the entertainment that was to follow, Katherine began.

"I promise to tell the whole story of the illustrious Bell Witch legend," which drew intense applause from the small group.

"But . . ." Katherine held up a slim index finger. The preacher's daughter knew something was coming that would require effort on their part. "But what?" Maggie implored, correctly judging that the children might not like the cost of the tale.

"We always face a long, hard winter in the Smoky Mountains, and there is always a price to pay for a good performance. Right?"

She received a collective and disappointed "Right."

"So what do we have to do?" Maggie impatiently tapped her right foot in as much of a scolding manner as a seven-year-old raised in the Appalachian heritage was allowed to address to an adult. "We're going to tell the story over a period of time, each exciting segment one story line at a time." Katherine explained. "In this way we have a. . . . " The raven-headed schoolteacher searched for the right words.

"It sounds like you're saying we can have something like a drama club," Mary Jane excitedly interrupted, holding her arm straight up in the air and waving it frantically back and forth just like she would if they all were in class at their school, Pi Beta Phi. The excited girl instantly clamped a hand over her mouth and stared with a frozen face as she realized she had just interrupted her teacher and spoken without permission. Being as bold and rude as to interrupt your teacher, and in what this part of the country would feel to be a very rude manner, could probably be a reason to have to sit in the corner. Katherine simply smiled at the young girl, whose face had flushed because she was now thoroughly embarrassed.

"Go ahead, Mary Jane," Katherine allowed. "It seems that you and I may have a common interest." Mary Jane shrugged enough that her shoulder-length hair bounced against the shoulder pads in her blouse. "I think meeting and discussing anything other than what the other adults do when they get together will be fun," Mary Jane concluded, some of the blush fading from her high cheekbones. Katherine pushed forward, sensing that she had at last attracted the interest of her most-intelligent student. The teacher added, "We can meet and get to know each other. All of you know that I haven't been here in the community that long, only since the beginning of the school year this past September. Now it's January. It's time I got to know everyone . . . better."

Katherine waited for Seth and Andrew to join in and share

Mary Jane's enthusiasm, but they just sat there, cozy by the warming fire, content to be seated next to Mary Jane. Sensing that Katherine needed someone to prod all of the group's interest in this project—including the boys—if this extracurricular get-together was going to happen, Mary Jane forgot her embarrassment as she tried to help push the project along. Mary Jane noted that Andrew and Seth were still sitting there like big bumps on the log. "We'll have to spend a lot of time together," she said.

Seth and Andrew both sat bolt upright from their slouches as what Mary Jane was saying sunk in. Emboldened, Mary Jane smiled at her teacher and added in a scathing tone, looking haughtily at the two boys, "My father says that literature, even discussing something as simple as this ghost story and learning from it, is the way that all of mankind and human culture has separated from the other creatures of the Earth."

Although Andrew and Seth probably could not have cared less what Mary Jane's father thought about "human culture," they bit their tongues and grudgingly decided that this drama class would be a way that they could spend extra time with Mary Jane. So the two did not say a word in opposition.

"All right then," Katherine nodded her head approvingly, and looked back and forth at her young audience. The slim young schoolteacher walked to the window overlooking the snow-laden mountains. Katherine looked longingly out at the pristine view that danced in the moonlight.

The lone black bat that had circled the building previously continued to swoop and swirl above the chimney.

"Vows," Katherine muttered under her breath. Then the teacher turned from the window and said, "Yes Maggie, Seth, Mary Jane and Andrew, a drama club," Kate acknowledged. She turned to look wistfully out the window at the scene that unfolded so beautifully.

"Why can't we just hear the story tonight . . . and act it out or whatever you do in a Drama Club . . . and be done with it!" Seth exclaimed. "That's why we all came up here anyway. To hear Miss Katherine's story of the Bell Witch legend."

"Yeah," Andrew agreed, looking over at Seth and nodding his head. "Why take more time that we could be doing other things that are more fun." Maggie quit toying with her blonde curls long enough to playfully smack the closest boy, which happened to be Seth, in the stomach with her opened right hand. "Shut up, both of you." The feisty little blonde giggled.

"If Miss Katherine wants us to do this, then we need to do this." Maggie nodded her head with enough authority to make her blonde curls bounce emphatically. Katherine continued to look out over the landscape of the cold night, pulling the drape away from the window.

"Thank you Maggie." Katherine acknowledged the youngster's enthusiasm. Then with a subdued voice and a far-off stare that almost appeared trance-like: "Maggie, you see, Mary Jane's father is right." Katherine talked slowly with a low voice, her breath causing a slight film of moisture to condense on the cold pane of glass each time she spoke. She explained in an almost-hushed voice, "In a drama club, one studies the bases for human actions and emotions."

Katherine's eyes seemed to glaze over and her stare began to look as if she were viewing things in her far-away past. "Oh yes, in a drama club we try to understand why people treat each other the way they do," Katherine continued. Letting out a barely audible sigh, the school marm spoke in her low monotone, as if she were alone. "Why does one man steal from another? What makes revenge so. . . . " Katherine's voice trailed off.

Seth and Andrew rolled their eyes in indifference at the low ramblings of their raven-haired schoolteacher who seemed to be talking nonsense that only Mary Jane seemed to appreciate. Nevertheless, their rolling eyes and lack of excitement was more at the prospect of meeting again and again on perfectly good evenings that would better used for hunting squirrels or raccoons or wandering around the mountains than discussing this ghost tale. Still, the boys reasoned . . . Mary Jane would be there.

"I think this is a wonderful idea," Mary Jane chimed in, slinging her long hair ever so slightly to emphasize that she wanted to have the drama club. With that, Seth and Andrew muttered, "Well, okay."

"Just okay, young men." Katherine stopped her low muttering. She briskly turned and walked away from the window, then plopped down on the chair in front of her youthful group.

"This is a great way to understand human actions. And again, Mary Jane's dad is right. A way to learn to grow, to escape your surroundings here in the Smoky Mountains and to understand others."

Mary Jane held up her hand excitedly again. "Shakespeare looked into the human condition as well as any other writer before or since. That's what we could learn in the drama club about the Bell Witch! We could look at, and learn about, the human conditions from this legend of long ago."

Even though Mary Jane was mature beyond her years, she was still a child. And being a child, she was not above showing off her knowledge in front of her peers. Especially when it came to making Seth and Andrew look young and immature. She couldn't help it. Mary Jane got a special kick out of putting the two in their place. Especially Andrew, because he was spoiled. His dad owned much of the town, and the boy was always being catered to because of what his family had, not what Andrew knew or deserved. Andrew constantly let the small group of his peers know that he was always treated special because of his family's financial status.

Mary Jane did like to tease Seth, too. But to be honest, it was because of the small crush she had on the son of the local ne'er-do-well, not the pleasure she received from teasing the lazy and spoiled Andrew.

Katherine looked down upon the young beauty; her gaze was direct and forceful. The strength and penetrating nature of Kate's gaze actually put a shiver in Mary Jane that she couldn't understand or easily shake off.

"Why yes, Mary Jane," Katherine slowly said, still staring at Mary Jane so directly that Mary Jane had to avert her eyes to get away from the intensity of her teacher's stare.

Katherine quietly rose from her chair and walked over to Mary Jane, still seemingly enthralled. An unnerved Mary Jane sat as still as she could and didn't flinch when Katherine touched her head and began to slowly stroke her beautifully brushed, long blonde hair perfectly parted with small brown combs that had belonged to her dead mother.

"Such insight from someone so young is very, very unusual." Katherine stated in a voice so slightly above a whisper, as she continued to stroke the young girl's golden-blonde hair. The teacher took care to make sure that every strand of hair that had been jostled out of place during the children's rambunctious pleading was back in place. But Mary Jane noticed that not once did Katherine touch one of her mother's hair combs. The stroking was done in loving manner, but with a touch that made Mary Jane shiver. The others noticed the attention Mary Jane was getting, and it was special enough that Seth caught Mary Jane's eye and mouthed the words "teacher's pet."

Then abruptly, Katherine stepped back, and with a big smile on her face, she clapped her hands together twice. "This is the best thing that has happened to me since I came to the mountains five months ago." Katherine said, smiling broadly, suddenly relaxed. "Other than teaching at Pi Beta Phi, of course," she said.

Katherine's abrupt change of attitude put Mary Jane back at ease, and she instantly decided she had been imagining things in the way the teacher had touched her hair and stared at her. Mary Jane knew she had an active imagination at times, and it was this imagination that kept her happy with her life in Gatlinburg. Still, later on Mary Jane would subconsciously remember the unease she had felt from Katherine's touch that evening. Mary Jane's excitement for learning about the Bell Witch temporarily made her clammy feeling of a few moments earlier disappear. Her true enthusiasm lay in thinking about studying the story line, forming a drama club, studying the acting and discussing how Shakespeare might have influenced the telling of this Tennessee ghost story. There were a lot of the Shakespearean elements in the Bell Witch legend, Mary Jane romanticized. After all, Shakespeare had affected virtually all English legends and stories and plays, whether people knew it or not. Her father had enough interest in literature and the arts to explain to his young daughter that educated people recognized the playwright as a tremendous influence on written and verbal cultures that had passed down through the years. So the Bell Witch story was intriguing in a way, but it was the acting, writing and drama classes that held Mary Jane's interest even more.

Mary Jane loved her father, and she enjoyed her life in the Smoky Mountains. Having spent only a few months of her young life there, she knew she had found home. Sometimes, Mary Jane even dreamed of settling down with a nice mountain boy in a few more years. However, the thought of marrying someone like Andrew Reagan was appalling to her soul. Seth

Sells was the most suitable boy she had met so far whom she could have even considered the thought of marrying. Seth had already told Mary Jane his thoughts of how noble he believed it to be to practice medicine like his hero, Dr. Thomas. Mary Jane had imagined that she could accept this way of life. A doctor's wife in the Smokies would be admired and deferred to, so this kind of existence would not be intolerable. Besides, Seth was not only cute, but he already displayed the traits that Mary Jane knew would guarantee he'd not follow in his no-good father's footsteps.

However, the young Mary Jane also had a mirror and eyes. She knew that she was pretty and fantasized about being a Hollywood starlet on the silver screen. What female born in the U.S. of A. had not dreamed of being swept off her feet by Clark Gable, and transported to the live in Beverly Hills or Hollywood. Rhett . . . or Clark . . . had done this exact same thing to Vivian Leigh in Gone With the Wind, why not her? Now this was Mary Jane's idea of a dream come true. Why couldn't this happen for her, too? Her pretty young teacher Katherine was going to have a drama class, telling stories and explaining how legend, history, love stories, family tradition and yes, even ghost stories meld together, just like Shakespeare did with some of his most famous masterpieces. Mary Jane saw that she could learn and study all of that right here in the mountains. She didn't have to go anywhere. Maybe they were going to discuss what happened with the legend of the Bell Witch, instead of Shakespeare's play, but who cared? It beat learning about how to make lye soap and washing out grass stains from a youngster's Levi's or darning socks.

It was a start. It was going to be fun, different and exciting. It would be a break from the boring mountain routines. True, Mary Jane thought the mountains to be majestically beautiful. Especially when they were "smoking" like they did for the Cherokees who named them. The bejeweled Smokies were glorious, and if she eventually settled down with someone like Seth, that was okay. Mary Jane knew that the motion picture life was probably never going to happen for someone like her. Still, to broaden her perspective with a little knowledge of something outside of her routine was invigorating. Mary Jane had learned that from her pop. Jake Bell wanted to have a new life after his wife died, and he did so. He packed up his young daughter and moved from the Nashville basin, eventually arriving at the spectacular views of the Smoky Mountains, a whole new way of life and a fresh beginning.

Mary Jane knew she probably was overly excited about learning an old ghost tale from her teacher, but she figured that was okay. Life had been pretty mundane, so what was the harm in allowing herself to be carried away by learning more about a legend that every schoolchild in Tennessee knew pretty much by heart. Mary Jane Bell found herself smiling inwardly, and then this smile slowly manifested itself externally. Mary Jane allowed herself to smile broadly and to show her enthusiasm for hearing the legend of the Bell Witch. Although her teacher was not as pretty as the youngster, she had her charms. Katherine was pleased, despite her previous protests to the opposite, that her students wanted to learn about Tennessee's most notorious witch. Katherine was especially pleased that she seemed to have attracted Jake Bell's daughter's rapt attention. Katherine smiled back at her delightfully appealing young protégé. As her smile beamed broadly, her subtle but alluring beauty bubbled to the surface. Katherine's captivating beauty, which she did not want to show to most of the mountain folk, suddenly came through, impressing the young Mary Jane. Though mature for her years, she was still impressionable, as all are at her age.

Katherine's smile grew broader, showing her pleasure

with her student taking such an interest in her story-telling and teaching ability. Her teacher's sudden attractiveness was something new to Mary Jane. To her, it made Katherine's previous, mostly simple, mundane life seem to melt away a bit too, no matter how frigid it was still outside.

Mary Jane thought her teacher's beauty seemed to grow as the loud cracking fire flamed up. The red glowing oak embers seemed to Mary Jane to make Katherine's homespun dress suddenly appear almost glamorous.

Katherine's smile soon matched the smile that Mary Jane wore. The schoolteacher had done exactly what she wanted to do on this cold, snowy night. Katherine had attracted Mary Jane's attention. Katherine hoped soon to capture Mary Jane's trust, as well.

CHAPTER 3

"I DON'T CARE, Rellie. I don't give one hoot what you say or think about her," Violla said to her henpecked husband of thirty-two years. "I don't like that school marm and that is it."

Rellie pulled another puff on his corncob pipe and answered as he usually did when his wife started a one-way conversation: "Yes, dear, whatever you say, Violla dear," not daring to glance up at the squat, sturdy Violla, still shaking her head to illustrate her intense displeasure.

Violla continued on her unremitting diatribe, "And I don't like the way she has her eyes on the glassblower, Jake Bell. The whole community thinks that fine-looking man ought to marry my sister, Hattie, and you know it, Rellie!"

Rellie took a brief break from his pipe and had a sip of courage from the small bottle of corn squeezings he kept hidden in his boot. Displaying a rare bit of intestinal fortitude imparted by his third gulp of the corn liquor, he said, "Now Violla dear, Jake will make up his mind, and your sister is right near twenty-three years older than Craftsman Bell. Maybe we ought to stay out of this, Vi my darling." He always called her Vi when he sensed an argument heading his way.

SPLAT! A just-out-of-the-oven corn muffin sailed one inch

above Rellie's slicked-back gray hair and landed with such force on the wall behind him that one of the dozen pictures of Violla's beloved sister Hattie fell to the floor.

"See what you done made me do; you caused me to break one of the pictures!" she exclaimed.

"Oh, Violla, behave yourself, little sister," came the soft, self-assured voice of her oldest sister, Rhode. Short for Rhododendron, the mountain flower, Rhode's name was an ideal illustration of its owner. If there ever was such a thing as a name being a perfect fit, it was Rhododendron. Their mother had thought so much of the beautiful flowering mountain plant that she had to name a daughter after it. Of course, the nickname Rhode stuck because Rhododendron is such a mouthful.

In these parts of the Smoky Mountains, it was generally known that Rhode was special. Smart, courageous and knowledgeable, she was an inspiration to all the God-fearing mountain women because she left her cozy home and ventured further south for many years to study the teachings of Jesus Christ at seminary. Rhode was looked up to as a sort of a community and even spiritual leader, respected more than some preachers. She knew the land and its people and was beloved by all. Rhode's faith was solid and never wavering. She had built her house not on the sand, but on the rock.

Rellie heaved a sigh of relief as he bent over, his big belly busting out of his overalls, to pick up the glass from Hattie's broken picture. Rhode was the only person that could make Violla behave. Not even the Sheriff could make her mind. She could cuss a mean streak and wrestle with the best of any mountain man, but one look from Rhode would set her straight.

Rellie smiled to himself as he gathered up the shards of glass and placed them on the small black-and-white photo of poor Hattie, musing that she was quite possibly the most common-looking woman in the mountains. Violla didn't see it, but everyone else knew why Hattie had not attracted a man. Violla couldn't stand the thought of her sister being alone. This intense desire to match her sister up with an eligible man was Violla's reason to survive.

As for Rhode, her husband had died in a horrible accident hiking up to Clingman's Dome many years before. Their love was deep, and Rhode never remarried. She found solace in the Lord and fervently studied theology.

Some people are pretty on the outside; some are pretty on the inside. People didn't pay much attention to the way Rhode looked, because she just exuded from inside a beauty that was so extraordinary, she was considered physically beautiful as well. And she was, in her own natural way. She had long graying hair that was always combed beautifully and parted perfectly in the middle.

Rhode had that communication with God and the land, and all of the mountain people thought she was perfect. Perhaps one shouldn't describe any person as perfect, but when people spoke of her, they didn't mention that she was perfect, but they just innately knew it. And this was understood by all in the mountains.

After Rhode had stepped in the clapboard house, she bent over to help Rellie pick up the broken glass that had just moments before covered the likeness of her other sister, Hattie.

"Now tell me, what brought all of this commotion about?" Rhode asked quietly of her sister Violla. Rhode reached over with her right hand and patted Rellie on his forearm, giving him comfort for his patience, as she also reached for some glass scattered on the floor with her left hand.

"I can't help it, Rhode," Violla exclaimed, her voice showing she was becoming agitated again. The veins in her short thick neck began to pop out like ropes.

"Calm down now, Violla," Rhode cautioned again, smiling at her sister and putting the last piece of broken glass onto the crumpled face of Hattie, staring back at her from the old photo.

Violla collapsed in her chair in the kitchen. After Rellie had dumped the broken glass into the trash can, Violla grabbed the crumpled photo from his hand.

Frantically shaking her unsmiling sister's picture back and forth in the air over her head, Violla began to explain to Rhode what had gotten her into such a foul mood.

"This teacher comes to our beautiful mountain community," Violla started.

"Nothing unusual about that, Violla," Rhode said in her calming voice, trying to help Violla keep her temper under control. "Sorry I interrupted you; go ahead and continue."

"Well, why should this one visitor come to our town, settle in and well, to be honest, be accepted as the teacher in our school and steal our sister's beau."

"Violla, Jake Bell could hardly be called our sister's beau. She just sat next to him during the church's Thanksgiving dinner." By now the two sisters had joined Rellie at the small round oak table that sat in the corner of the small kitchen. Rellie returned to puffing on his corncob pipe, now that the hurricane named Violla had been downgraded to a mere tropical depression. He began to ruminate on, well, whatever Rellie ruminated every other day of the year that he had to endure his life.

"You must be more accepting of outsiders, my dear sister Violla," Rhode continued, as she patted her hand, which still held the crumpled picture of the insulted, impugned, violated and disgraced Hattie. Violla sat with the picture of her sister and big tears formed in both eyes. No matter whatever faults Violla had, she loved her two sisters. She loved them more than just about anything else in the world. Many years ago, Rellie had hoped to be surrounded by that special type of love, but he had given up and sunk into the flask of white lightning that nestled in his rawhide boot and was his constant companion.

"You have so much more love in you, Sister Rhode, than I do." Violla's tears had now begun to flow fairly steadily, and they rolled off her rounded bulldog face onto the oaken table.

"Oh, that's not true at all, sister Violla," Rhode patted her sister's arm ever more affectionately.

"Remember when I had the opportunity to study at the seminary down in New Orleans, next to Tulane University. I received a whole lot of insight into the ways of our Lord Jesus Christ when I studied there. I became humble. I studied as hard as I could to learn the truth and the power and beauty of our Savior and the compassion in the ways of the Lord." That seemed to make Violla feel some better, as her tears stopped flowing. "That's right, Rhode, you did, didn't you? You're the same as the Reverend Cane down at First Methodist; you know what the Lord wants us to do." Violla now was feeling much better. "Please help me help sister Hattie, Rhode. She needs to be hitched to a man so bad," Violla continued, rubbing her eyes and nose with the back of her wrist. "She's so all alone, Rhode," Violla continued. "And she's such a pretty little thing," Violla insisted. Rellie choked on his last slug of corn liquor when Violla described the beauty of her old maid sister Hattie. Even Rhode had to stifle a bit of a chuckle to hear her sister Hattie described in such glowing physical terms.

"Well, we really don't know the craftsman Mr. Bell and his family very well, do we? We don't see them except on Sundays at the church. We ought to go pay them a visit."

"We will someday," Rellie piped up, "but now I have some chores to do around the house."

"Chores? Rellie, you haven't done any chores around here, since. . . ." Violla tried to remember her henpecked husband having done anything productive around the house, which made her even more flustered.

Rellie had slunk away from the table to escape the avalanche of verbal abuse headed his way. He had gotten almost to the front door to make his escape when he heard his wife command, "Rellie, you aren't going anywhere."

"Now Violla, don't be so hard on Rellie," Rhode interrupted. Rellie breathed a little sigh of relief and pushed back his slicked-back hair around his graying and thinning temples. "But Rellie, Violla is right. We should be ashamed of ourselves. Jake Bell and his daughter Mary Jane have been part of the community for a while now. We don't know them except for church. There's no time like the present to go meet one's obligations," his sister-in-law said.

Rellie didn't say another word; he walked over to the closet by the front door he had hoped to use as his escape. He opened the closet door and pulled out his wool overcoat, handed Violla hers.

"It's cold outside, so we have to wrap up." Violla smiled a big broad smile and waltzed over to the outstretched coat that Rellie had waiting for her. Violla graciously allowed her husband to place the old black coat around her broad shoulders, helping her to put her arms through the sleeves, just as a gentleman should. Rellie knew that if Rhode said it was time to do something, it was going to be done, so there was no use in fighting it.

"Where exactly do they live?" Rellie asked when the threesome packed into the old Model T that Rellie had morphed into a truck with a hacksaw and a whole lot of baling wire. It was ridiculous-looking, but it served its purpose, toting Rellie around the Smoky Mountains while he drank.

"The glassblower Bell and his daughter are over on River Road at the old Brewer place," Rhode said, motioning for Rellie to start the car and get going.

"Dave Brewer left?" Rellie asked, a bewildered look on his face.

Thump. Violla hit Rellie over the head with her small black purse, which looked as if it had been made out of a sow's ear.

"Ow!" Rellie barked. "What's that fer?"

"Dave Brewer died five years ago."

Rellie fired up the old car and clanged the gears back and forth until he found reverse. He pulled back a few yards and then off they went. Rellie had lashed a large barrel onto the back of the car, which he always kept filled with water. Rellie's premise was that during winter, he needed the weight of the water barrel to give him traction in the ice and snow. True, the bad roads and bad winter weather in the mountains meant that any vehicle needed extra traction to get from one hollow to the next peak to the next hollow. It made Rellie seem a little less ridiculous to the town folk, who had an erstwhile explanation for the enormous barrel. The people who really knew Rellie were not fooled. Rellie had been known to carry around an old still for producing white lightning for Johnson Sells. It was a perfect fit. Rellie would slide the still inside the big barrel and then off he would go, carrying the illegal liquor machine to another hiding place right before the Revenuers could catch him.

Rellie had taken the still out tonight, and had replaced it with water since traction was actually needed because of the inclement weather. The water was ice-cold, and when Rellie hit the brakes, the filled-to-the-brim-barrel emptied a good deal of its frigid contents. Rellie had, through the years, cracked or broken all of the windows in the old Model T. For some reason, he had never replaced them. So as the frigid water came cascading forward toward the front of the car, a goodly amount of icy cold water splashed through the missing back window. A collective "Oh My God" was screamed by Rhode, Violla and even Rellie as the near-freezing liquid splashed on their backs. Even the ever even-keeled Rhode could not prevent the purse lashing that Violla gave Rellie that evening.

"Rellie," Violla screamed at the top of her lungs, as she repeatedly thumped Rellie over his head with her sow's ear purse. "If you don't replace the windows in this here car, like most normal people would, I am going to give you a whatever like you have never ever received," Violla yelled. She gave Rellie one last especially hard slap on the mouth to emphasize her point.

The ride to Jake Bell's glass-blowing shop, which was going to be cool at best due to Rellie's special Model T air conditioning, was now made almost unbearably cold by the ice-cold slosh that was trying to freeze on Rhode, Violla and Rellie. The old heater in the Model T helped some, but not much.

The road to Jake Bell's home passed right by Gatlinburg's Pi Beta Phi school. While Rellie and Violla were trying to flick the ice out of their hair and off their clothes, Rhode paid special attention to the darkened school and the two-story log cabin home set off about a hundred yards where the new teacher lived. Rhode did not know much about Katherine, but she was interested to learn more. Being childless, Rhode had never really taken a huge interest in the Pi Beta Phi school; she was more interested in the local library, which surprisingly provided a great deal of information on her theological studies, which she dearly loved, almost to an obsessed level.

"Look at that!" Rhode blurted out, as she noticed a vaporous green light slinking along the white frozen ground from the school to Katherine's house.

"Look at what?" Rellie and Violla asked.

"Oh . . . er. . . . " Rhode pointed out a peculiar star formation close to the Northern Star in order to deflect the attention of Violla and Rellie from the green-tinted fog that had now disappeared into the teacher's house.

A single black bat floated high above the house, darting in and out of the night shadows, trying not to be seen.

Just before both Rellie and Violla were going to ask Rhode to let them turn around because of the cold, Rhode pointed to a dim light emanating from a small log home up the curving road.

"I do believe we have finally made it to the Bell home," Rhode proclaimed, dusting some last ice from sister Violla's eyebrows.

Rellie slowed down with great care as he approached Jake Bell's place. The water level in the barrel was not so low that a drenching would not happen again if he decelerated as he had before. And Rellie figured that he could not stand another icing or another flogging.

When the Model T did come to a stop in front of Jake Bell's establishment, the tall, thin gentleman who had created the beautiful glass items inside presented himself. With the front door opened, a wash of warm light emanated from his home.

"Good evening, Violla, Rellie. . . ." he said, squinting to see who the other passenger was. "Oh and Miss Rhode," Jake exclaimed as he saw Rhode exiting the Model T. "What good reason do I owe this visit?" Jake Bell asked, trying to mask the puzzled look on his face. Having visitors in the small mountain community was not that strange, but unannounced and in the cold of night like this was rather unexpected, if not unusual. "Oh, we felt we had been rude, Mr. Bell, not to have gotten to know you and your daughter better since you've arrived in our beautiful mountains. And we thought it would be more neighborly to visit with you and your daughter some to get to know ye better," Rhode announced.

Jake couldn't help but giggle to himself a bit as he noticed that all three had ice dripping from their hair and clothing. "Please excuse my rudeness," Jake exclaimed, as he motioned the threesome into his warm home. "My daughter and I have not had many visitors, and I believe I have forgotten my manners. It must be terribly cold tonight driving in an open car such as yours."

That gave Violla another reason to whack Rellie on the shoulder with her sow's ear purse as she began to explain to Jake Bell how the ice-cold water had sloshed into the Model T from the old barrel that was attached to the frame.

Once all had entered into the cozy log building, the three began to warm immediately. Although Jake's prized glass objects were mostly on display in the small log building attached to the home, hundreds of glass-blown objects littered his home.

"Mary Jane!" Jake called for his young daughter to come down and meet their visitors. Soon, Mary Jane, with her brown combs holding her perfectly adorned blonde hair, hustled from her upstairs bedroom and presented herself.

"You remember these kind people from church, don't you daughter?' Jake asked.

"Yes sir," Mary Jane responded as she posed a small curtsy to all three and then boldly walked up to Rellie, Violla and Rhode and, in a manner befitting a young adult, shook hands with all three.

"Forgive my manners," Mary Jane declared, as she noted the icicles dangling from her visitors. "I will fix something warm from the kitchen. Perhaps hot cocoa for everyone?" The thought of a hot drink elicited a trio of "thank you" from the three frozen visitors. Especially Rellie, as he patted his boot to check on the silver flask hidden there.

As Mary Jane went into the small kitchen to prepare warming cocoa for all, Jake Bell motioned for his visitors to sit down on an old, worn sofa.

"Thank you for your hospitality, Mr. Bell," Rhode gushed as she stretched her hands in front of her still-cold torso, welcoming the warmness of the fire in the old limestone fireplace.

"Please, all of you, call me Jake; Mr. Bell is my father!" he chuckled and smiled at all three of his visitors.

Mary Jane returned with cups of cocoa for everyone almost before the visitors could even settle in and get comfortable.

"Amazing," Rhode said as she accepted her large steaming cup of cocoa from Mary Jane.

"Yes, isn't she amazing?" Jake Bell exclaimed with pride as Mary Jane served everyone like a little adult. "Oh . . . oh . . . yes, Mary Jane is amazing," Rhode stumbled around for the correct words as Jake had misconstrued her meaning for the word amazing. Rhode set down the cup of hot chocolate to pick up a small, hand-blown glass figurine of a mountain lion, one of the dozens of objects that were near the couch.

"Oh, oh," Jake nodded his head in affirmation, understanding that he had misidentified the reason for the praise. "Yes, the illusive Smoky Mountain puma or mountain lion is one of the best sellers in my shop." Rhode set down the prized glass figurine and took another sip of the chocolate drink that was warming all of the visitors.

"But I also agree with you, Mr. Bell," Rhode changed her wording to "Jake" when she noticed the young man's wagging finger. "Mary Jane is an incredible young woman."

"I am proud of my daughter," Jake Bell agreed as he pulled Mary Jane close to him and stroked her hair affectionately, taking particular care with the brown combs that were featured prominently in her hair. "And she's looking more like her mother every day." Jake seemed to instantly regret even bringing up his late wife's memory as a sad look came over his face. Rhode prepared to state in a more eloquent and detailed manner how she and her family, actually, everyone in the community, had felt bad because they all did not know more about Jake and Mary Jane.

Violla blurted out, "Mr. Bell, we come to find out your intentions toward our sister, the lovely and unmarried Hattie!" Clunk! The large white porcelain cup that Jake Bell had been drinking from actually slipped from his grip and hit the wooden floor beneath his feet.

"Violla!" Rhode declared as she sat up on the couch and swatted her sister on the hand in an attempt to show remorse for them both and to calm her sister's vaunted temper. Rhode then politely went over and picked up Jake's dropped cup from the floor. Handing it to Mary Jane, Rhode cooed, "Mary Jane, darling, will you be so kind as to fetch your father a refill? My well-meaning, but brash sister has caused your father to spill most of his refreshment." She smiled down at the also-stunned daughter. Then Rhode took a handkerchief out of her coat pocket and cleaned up the small amount of hot chocolate that had spilled.

"Well . . . well. . . ." Jake Bell stammered, hoping that Rhode would change the subject. But Rhode didn't say anything more as she took her seat next to her sister, the still jut-jawed, bulldoggish sister who apparently wanted to know his intentions toward a woman he barely remembered, much less had courted.

"I'm just really not over my wife yet. . . ." Jake stammered, not really knowing what to say. This was none of these people's business, but since he was new to the community he didn't want to blurt out what he really thought of Violla's question.

Jake was glad when Mary Jane brought the refill of hot chocolate from the kitchen and handed it to him. It allowed him to regain his composure and not demand that this group of people leave his home.

Jake drew Mary Jane close to him as he looked his visitors in the eye. "This is my special lady now. Mary Jane is the only lady that I even want to think of being in my family now." There, Jake Bell sighed to himself, he had diplomatically defused a situation in a way that would not offend anyone.

Violla took a large gulp from the dainty porcelain cup and grunted, "Then what is it between you and Katherine, the teacher woman then?"

This time Jake Bell held on firmly to his cup of cocoa, since he had already been broadsided by the outlandish nature of Violla's questions. Before Jake could say anything, Rhode grabbed Violla by the hand in a manner that showed she was going to gain control of her boorish sister.

"Violla! That's enough! We did not come here to offend Mr. Bell and his lovely daughter or to ask of him things that are none of our business." Before Rhode could continue in her conciliatory discourse, Violla interrupted her.

"Well, I came here to find out some answers to some questions that have been going around about Mr. Bell for months in this community!" Violla stated emphatically.

"I assure you, Violla," Jake Bell decided he would have to be proactive and change the conversation or he was going to lose his temper, "I have no romantic intentions toward your sister Hattie or Miss Katherine, the school marm." Regaining his composure and realizing that he did not need to offend his new neighbors, no matter how rude they were, he recognized that he needed to be diplomatic in his actions at all cost. Jake Bell again nodded toward his daughter Mary Jane. "Mary Jane's well being is really my only concern at this time in my life."

"Well, if you ain't interested in school marm Katherine, what's a good looking fella like you doing wanting to stay single when a lady as handsome as our sister Hattie is available?!" Before Rhode could interrupt her sister, she continued. "Why, Hattie is strong as an ox; she can push the bellows on that glass-blowing furnace so hard that you can turn out twice the amount of these glass things!" Violla declared.

"Violla!" Rhode nearly shouted, as she realized that Violla was ranting, almost out of control. The veins on her neck had now begun to pop out from her enthusiasm. Because of her sister's rudeness, Rhode had no choice but to break up the small gathering much earlier than she wanted to and take leave of Jake Bell and Mary Jane. Violla was flabbergasted when Rhode declared that the evening was over with and that she, Rellie and Violla needed to go home early to attend to other affairs.

"Why, we do not need to go home early!" Violla protested, as she was intent on getting answers from Jake Bell. After this, Rhode literally pulled her sister and Rellie off the couch.

"It was good to have you visit," Jake Bell lied as he showed these people he barely knew to the door of his home. He bravely smiled but was unable to utter the neighborly refrain so common in the mountains: "Ya'll come again." Rellie tried to get in a little business when he shook Jake's hand. Pulling the whiskey flask from its hiding place, he flashed it to Jake. "I got the best corn squeezings in the mountains if you ever need some, Mr. Bell."

"Thank you Rellie, I'll keep you in mind." Jake smiled politely.

Just as he turned to enter the warmth and dignity of his log home, Rhode turned around and approached him before he closed the door. Rhode leaned up to his ear and whispered in a tone only they could hear. "Vengeance, Mr. Bell," Rhode whispered so lightly in Jake's ear he was unclear if he had heard anything at all. "Just as with your great-great grandfather, John, the Bell Witch seeks vengeance and she means to have it."

Before a stunned Jake Bell could say anything, Rhode had pulled away from him. She threw her long white hair back over her shoulder, and while Jake tried to find his voice, Rhode traipsed over the snow-covered yard. She got into the Model T Ford, and she, Violla and Rellie pulled away in the sputtering vehicle and disappeared down the snowy road.

Far above in the frozen night sky, circling unseen was a single black bat. It could have been discerned in the moonlight if one were looking for it. But the creature was so small and silent that, this night, it flew unnoticed above the Jake Bell home.

"Vengeance." The word echoed through Jake's mind.

CHAPTER 4

"YOU KNOW, I'VE decided that we shouldn't tell anyone about our little drama class," Katherine explained to Seth, Andrew and Mary Jane. The small group had decided to meet in the basement of their school building in the village. It was close to everyone and it was open to the teacher.

Maggie, the little blonde, was absent. Her father, the good Reverend Cane, had decided his daughter shouldn't attend the telling of the Bell Witch.

"Yeah, my aunt. Or at least my family calls her my aunt," Seth began to speak and then decided that maybe his words would be out of place. Growing a bit flustered, Seth squirmed in his chair and decided to keep his mouth shut.

The entire group turned around and looked at Seth, awaiting whatever he was going to say. Still he kept his mouth shut.

"Go ahead and speak what's on your mind," Katherine urged.

Again, Seth hesitated but then decided to go ahead and speak up. "Well, my Aunt Rhode. . . ." Seth hesitated again when he saw his teacher's face scrunch up in disdain with the mention of Rhode's name. "Go ahead," Katherine said, trying in vain to hide her disgust. "Tell us what your Aunt Rhode had to say," Katherine spat out. Andrew and Mary Jane discreetly looked at each other with concern and curiosity. They had never heard Katherine ever say anything like this. They didn't know that she even had met Seth's Aunt Rhode. Evidently she had, and obviously she didn't care for her. This was a part of their youthful, vibrant teacher that Andrew, Seth and Mary Jane had never seen before. It actually scared them a bit. The distraught Seth started to stumble on his words, and he actually stuttered a bit. He squirmed a bit more in his seat, now regretting that he had ever opened his big mouth.

Trying to hide her anger, Katherine said again, "Go ahead, Seth, let's hear what that old windbag Rhode had to say."

"Well," Seth began, still very uncertain that he should even repeat what his Aunt Rhode had told him. Seth looked over at the waiting Mary Jane and realized he was looking like a fool with his stuttering and stumbling. What could the harm be in telling everyone what his Aunt Rhode had to say? He decided to continue.

"Rhode said maybe we should study something else."

"Like what?" Katherine spat out. Again Andrew and Mary Jane looked at each other; it was obvious that Katherine didn't approve of Seth's aunt and would not enjoy whatever else Seth would have to say.

Andrew looked at Seth and tried to silently suggest, "Why don't you just be quiet?" It didn't work. Seth continued. "Well . . . Rhode said maybe we should study Shakespeare instead of the legend of the Bell Witch," Seth said, then he had enough presence of mind just to shut up, momentarily. Then, strangely and quite mysteriously, Katherine's demeanor changed altogether.

"Perhaps your aunt is right, Seth. Maybe we should study something more traditional, such as Shakespeare or some other American literary legend like Poe."

Mary Jane and Andrew nodded their heads in agreement. Oh, they still wanted to hear the legend of the Bell Witch. Now even more than ever since Katherine's reaction had been so strong at the mention of Seth's Aunt Rhode. It was as if he had mentioned poison. Rhode must have done something to really offend their teacher, and they couldn't wait to hear it. The kids just knew tonight probably wasn't the appropriate time to push.

You know, though, Seth still didn't seem to get it. He had to say something else. He just had to. Even though he was uncomfortable with himself, he couldn't help it.

"Rhode said we shouldn't hear this story because it might upset Mary Jane."

"Me!" Mary Jane spoke out in surprise. "I know that I have the last name Bell, but my father assured me the other night that we didn't have anything to do with this legend."

"Is that what he said? Is it?" Katherine asked, an eyebrow lifting high on her forehead. This look was enough that Mary Jane decided to shut her mouth and just sit there and be quiet. When she was preoccupied, like now, Mary Jane would instinctively touch her beautiful long hair and move her combs through her hair. The young girl was distracted enough to start doing just that. Mary Jane thoughtfully took the brown combs from her blonde hair and started to straighten her tresses.

Seth wouldn't leave it alone, though. "Yeah, Rhode said we wouldn't like the story and that it had a sad ending." Then Seth finally did something smart; he shut his mouth. But it was too late. The teacher's brow arched, making her dark hair seem to peak high over her head. The children didn't know it was a sign of anger, but it was. Now Katherine was going to simmer a bit inside. Instinctively, she began to show another side of herself, one that no one in the mountain hamlet had seen much of. Now the teacher Katherine was also a bit curious.

"So Jake Bell said the Bell Witch legend has ended, did he?" Katherine fairly purred. The school marm's question was quiet and almost gleeful.

"Do you know my father, teacher Katherine?" Mary Jane decided to speak up again.

Katherine laughed a laugh that, the truth be known, sent a shiver down all of the school kids' backs. It wasn't a normal laugh. Then just as quickly as their sweet schoolteacher had acted so unnaturally unpleasant, her normal demeanor reappeared. It was confusing to the mountain kids. Who was this lady? She had been their teacher for this school year, but did they really know her? What did this talk about someone's aunt she might not even know have to do with anything?

Finally, after what seemed a lifetime, Katherine answered Mary Jane's question. "Yes, I know your father," Katherine answered. But she spoke so quietly that it seemed as if she were telling a secret that shouldn't be told.

Mary Jane again was confused by all of this much ado about nothing. As far as she knew, her father had actually only spoken to Rhode once outside of church—at any rate they didn't know each other very well. Why would Rhode believe that hearing the legend of the Bell Witch would upset Mary Jane? But what was more disconcerting to Mary Jane was that Katherine seemed so interested in her father, Jake. Sure, they had probably met somewhere she wasn't aware of, such as a meeting or at church or something. However, it was the way that Katherine had responded that made her curious. Plus, this thing that Seth said about his Aunt Rhode wanting them not to talk about the Bell Witch legend. Hadn't her father said specifically that their family wasn't kin to the Bell family? If somehow her end of the Bell family tree was involved in this mysterious legend, she felt sure that her father would have told her. But something gnawed at her. Mary Jane knew she was deceiving herself a bit.

To be truthful to herself, Jake really didn't speak of his family, at all. The more these thoughts flashed through her mind, the more uneasy she became. Her father's family and her ancestors were a complete mystery to her. Mary Jane had an epiphany. She realized she didn't know anything at all about her family. As far as Mary Jane knew, she could be a relative of this John Bell that was the center of this Bell Witch legend.

Mary Jane realized she wanted to hear Katherine tell this witch story now more than ever. What if it did have to do with her? Was her father Jake involved with her teacher Katherine? Jake did go to some meetings and such alone. Was he actually courting Katherine and she didn't know it? Maybe that would explain why the teacher became so upset earlier. Before Mary Jane had time to say anything, Katherine spoke up in the most pleasant of voices. This was the teacher they had come to know.

"I believe there is probably a reason not to pursue this. Maybe Seth has a point." Then Katherine said something astute that almost put everyone at ease again. Almost.

"It was you children, after all, who wanted to hear this legend and form this drama club," the teacher said sweetly.

Mary Jane couldn't resist now. Curiosity had gotten the better of her anxiety. "No, go ahead, teacher Katherine!" Mary Jane declared just as Andrew was shaking his head "No." It was too late—Mary Jane spoke up again. "Please, we won't interrupt you again."

There was a long silence. Andrew and Seth sat there with absolutely nothing to say. Katherine just looked at Mary Jane. Mary Jane now didn't know what to say. Finally, Katherine responded, very quietly and deliberately. She turned and took up the eraser and slowly in circular motions erased the blackboard where the words "Bell Witch . . . A Tennessee Legend" had been written.

"If you children still want to hear about the Bell Witch, then I suggest we go about this differently." Katherine spoke so quietly with her back to them that they all had to strain to hear her.

"This Saturday night, at the abandoned Old Glory Holiness Church," Katherine spoke deliberately as she turned, clapping her hands together to shake the last remnants of chalk dust from her hands.

"The old church has a stage where I can give a perfect presentation," Katherine said sweetly. "If you children have an interest, then come down. I will speak of the Bell Witch legend as I know it and I will do it all in one night."

Now Andrew and Seth had overcome their discomfort as their curiosity began to overtake them. Say what they would about their teacher, there was something about Katherine that made you sit up in your chair and pay attention when she spoke as she did now.

"It probably is a better idea that we study the masters such as Shakespeare when we are here at school," she said as she swept her chalk-stained hand around the room. "I believe it will be more acceptable to hear my rendition of this unusual, and I must say, personal legend at the old church than anywhere else."

It is said that curiosity killed the cat. Well, curiosity certainly had captivated the children. Seth, Andrew and Mary Jane sat mesmerized. Long gone was the feeling of discomfort that they had felt earlier. It was replaced by a trance-like feeling that they would have to be there Saturday night, now more than ever, to hear this story.

"We'll be there," Mary Jane offered first. Then Seth and Andrew said that they would be there, too.

"Good, I'll see you then," Katherine declared as she cleaned her hands. And then with a swish of the long raven hair that flashed across her face, "Don't forget to lock up," the teacher said nonchalantly as she left the schoolhouse.

Seth, Andrew and Mary Jane were left dumbstruck. Finally Mary Jane said, "I'm going." Of course, what else could the boys say? They weren't about to be undone by this small girl.

"We'll be there, too," Seth and Andrew declared. "All right, then, it's decided: We'll all be there," Mary Jane said determinedly. "And by the way, Seth, what's the story on this Aunt Rhode of yours?" Mary Jane asked, with a hint of disdain. She suddenly had forgotten how uncomfortable they all had felt earlier that evening when their teacher was so upset by the mere mention of Seth's aunt. Seth was shy, and he knew he had messed up the entire evening by bringing up something that didn't matter anyway. Seth didn't know why Rhode's opinion had meant so much to Katherine, but now he was concerned that the girl he liked was mad at him. Seth had blundered terribly earlier that evening, and he knew it.

"Oh, never mind," Seth tried to wave off the distraction. Instead, he asked of his friends, "Are we all going to this séance, or whatever it is, Saturday night?"

"Séance?" Mary Jane repeated, mocking Seth, which embarrassed him even more.

"Whatever it is, I'll be there," Seth hurriedly replied, fearing that he had somehow upset Mary Jane more.

"Okay then," Mary Jane declared. "I'll see you guys Saturday night." And she started out the door, tugging on her warm overcoat.

"Don't you want me to walk you home?" Seth called out after her.

"No! I don't need anyone to walk me home. It's just a little ways from here. I'll be fine." With that Mary Jane skipped out of the room.

Andrew turned to Seth with a puzzled look on his face. "What in the world got into the teacher tonight?" he asked his friend. Seth sighed and asked, "Andrew, I know you like Mary Jane too, like every other guy around. Do you think I blew it with her tonight, looking like a fool like I did?"

"Naw, Seth, I don't think so," Andrew tried to reassure his good friend. "But what would I know, Seth?" Andrew said, laughing a bit. "I'm just a kid too!" Then they both laughed out loud together.

Mary Jane had decided to scurry home as fast as she could. She had determined that she had some very important questions she wanted to ask her father. She realized she knew fundamentally nothing of her own family. All she really knew was that her mother had died giving birth to her. Although Mary Jane was very young, she still felt guilty about that. She didn't know exactly why; it was confusing, but she did.

She pulled her hand-spun cloth coat closer against her to keep out the cold Smoky Mountain night. It was a lonely old road that led out to the houses where the craftspeople in town lived. It was gravel, and her small black shoes made a crunching sound along the way. Mary Jane started to walk a bit faster as she felt the cold mountain wind circle viciously around her. It gave the young lady a chill that she had not experienced before. Then, all of a sudden, something slipped into Mary Jane's subconscious mind. Someone was following her, or so she thought. Perhaps, she thought, it was just the biting wind that was scaring her.

She decided to walk a little faster still. Mary Jane couldn't shake the fact that she felt threatened and followed. There it was again. It was like her exact footsteps were being echoed back to her. She couldn't help it; her feet began to walk faster still. Yet no matter how fast or slow she walked, the steps from behind seemed to match hers exactly. Now, Mary Jane's heart began to beat wildly. It seemed to skip erratically, then beat wildly again as her terror grew and grew. Her shoes stamped out a faster beat on the crushed stone path. Blasts of cold breath escaped from her mouth. The rapidity of Mary Jane's breathing began to scare her. It hurt each time she took a deep gulp of the freezing night air.

Mary Jane's breath froze right in front of her face in the frigid night air. Her breath, turning into a curious white cloak that obscured her vision, scared her even more. "Ow!" Mary Jane yelled out, and wiped a hand on the back of her head where she felt a sharp sting. When she pulled her hand back and looked at it the silver moonlight, it was covered in bright red blood. Mary Jane stopped dead in her tracks. Her breath continued to explode from her mouth. She bent over at the waist and placed her hands on her knees as she sought to catch her breath. Then she looked up in the sky, and a lone black bat swooped and swished around in the moonlight. The bat must have attacked her, and left her scalp bleeding. She looked again at her bloody hand in disbelief.

Now Mary Jane was really in a panic. Not only was she injured, she could still sense the presence of someone following her. Mary Jane could feel her heart beating so hard in her chest, she thought anyone around might hear it. She was still breathing so hard that her frozen breath escaped from her mouth in bursts, rasping at her throat.

"AWWWW!" Mary Jane screamed as she suddenly bumped into a white-haired woman who stood in her path. Mary Jane wanted to run. But she was too panic-filled to do so. She was frozen with fear.

"Don't worry, Mary Jane Bell," the slight lady with the flowing white locks said.

"How do you know my name?" Mary Jane squeaked out, even though her voice was two octaves higher than normal.

"I know a lot of things," was all the lady said. When Mary Jane got a good look at the woman's face, her beating heart began to slow some. The face was gentle, and lined in a way that communicated innocence and purity.

"Here," the little lady said, as she took a handkerchief from her coat pocket and pressed it into the wound on the top of Mary Jane's head. "Ow!" Mary Jane complained as the lady continued to apply pressure to the still-bleeding wound. "That hurts!" Mary Jane complained again. The white-haired woman didn't stop; she kept attending to the wound.

It was Rhode. The kindly old woman who had visited her father's home only a few nights before. The same woman whom Seth called his aunt. Mary Jane couldn't explain why, but standing with Rhode in the moonlight made her feel safe.

Mary Jane's face brightened. "Seth has told us about you." Her breathing slowed, and her heart quit beating so wildly. "Something good, I hope?" the lady said as she continued to put pressure on the wound. Then she put her arms around Mary Jane's slight shoulders and pushed her forward along the path to the craft community, now only a hundred yards or so away.

"He really didn't say much about you other than that you were his aunt."

"Oh, I'm really not Seth's aunt; he's just called me that all of his life." Then Rhode looked down at Mary Jane and said, "Why are you walking alone this late at night? Does your father realize you are out this late?"

"Yes, he knows we had a class tonight, and he let me go alone. It's not far from the house."

"What did you learn at the school tonight?" Rhode asked as they walked along the lonely road, rustling leaves swirling around their feet. Mary Jane hesitated. "It's okay, Mary Jane. I'm just curious; you can tell me anything."

"Well . . ." Mary Jane stammered, but she was so soothed by the winsome old face of Rhode that she went on. "We learned that for some reason, our teacher, Miss Katherine, doesn't like you." Mary Jane immediately realized she had said too much.

"That's okay," Rhode stated. "She never has liked me very much."

Mary Jane got a confused look over her face, trying to understand how Rhode and Katherine could know each other, since Katherine had just moved to the Smoky Mountains earlier this year. Rhode kept gentle pressure on Mary Jane's head. "Actually, that was the reason I was walking behind you tonight. I wanted to talk with your dad, Jake."

"Why do you want to talk with my dad?" Mary Jane asked, now really confused.

"I have some information that I want to. . . ." Rhode now stumbled over her words as they turned up the driveway to the Bell home. "I just want to talk to your father some, nothing important, nothing to worry yourself about," Rhode stated gently.

Mary Jane led the way up on the porch and then pushed the door open. Rhode slipped by Mary Jane to the sink and pumped some water into a small bowl there. She began to clean the wound more thoroughly. "Where is your father?" Rhode asked as she finally removed the last bit of blood from Mary Jane's blonde hair.

"I'm right here," Jake Bell said.

"Father," Mary Jane beamed as she turned to her dad, very glad to see him.

"Mary Jane, what in the world happened to your head?" Jake asked as a worried look crossed his face. He stooped over to see the deep gash in his daughter's scalp. Jake reached for a lamp and brought it close to examine his daughter's wound.

"Good lord!" Jake exclaimed.

"A bat bit her," Rhode said solemnly.

"A bat?" Jake asked with a skeptical look on his face. "We're not in South America. There aren't any vampire bats in the United States, much less the Smoky Mountains, as far as I know."

"Oh, there are all sorts of weird occurrences that will happen now, Mr. Bell," Rhode said patiently, trying not to alarm Mary Jane.

Mary Jane saw Rhode and her father exchange a glance. It was a look that she had seen other grown-ups share before. It was a worried look that meant trouble. It made Mary Jane hurt in her stomach as she realized something was amiss, but she knew that her father would never, ever tell her. No matter how bad things were, Jake Bell never complained. He never let on to others, much less his daughter, about trouble. It just wasn't his style to complain or share worries with anyone else.

Jake heaved a heavy sigh as he nodded at Rhode, acknowledging that he understood. Then Jake Bell turned to Mary Jane. She thought her father had the saddest look on his face that she had ever seen before. Even sadder than when he would explain to Mary Jane about how much he loved her mother and how much it hurt to lose her. Mary Jane was so immersed in the forlornness of her father's face that she barely heard Jake say, "Are you all right now?"

Her father's voice jolted her back to reality.

"Yes, Father, it didn't hurt that much and Rhode has already cleaned it up." Mary Jane explained. Jake smiled kindly at his daughter. "Good then, go ahead and get ready for bed, Mary Jane."

"Why do I have to go to bed now? I want to talk to Rhode some," Mary Jane protested. Jake smiled softly and said, "Mary Jane, I need to talk with Rhode about some. . . ." He struggled to say the right words. "I need to talk with Rhode about some personal matters that will not involve you." Mary Jane hung her head. Even though she was mature for her age, she still was a child, and like all children, didn't want to go to bed while the adults stayed up talking.

"Go on now, Mary Jane," Jake stated again. "School will come early in the morning. Get on up to bed." Mary Jane reluctantly started up the steps to the loft above.

"Good night, Mary Jane. Be sure to keep your wound clean for the next few days," Rhode reminded her.

"Thank you, Rhode," Mary Jane mumbled as she took each step slowly, trying to listen to her father and Rhode's conversation. She paused at the last step, where they could not see her; Mary Jane leaned over as far as she could and tried to eavesdrop on the soft, intense words that Rhode was speaking rapidly. Mary Jane knew she heard the names "Rellie" and "Violla." Mary Jane heard the name "Katherine" and "evil"—or perhaps it was "anvil," since her father did keep two anvils to work on. Mary Jane leaned so far over that she slipped and fell down one step with a thud!

"Mary Jane!?!" Jake Bell took leave of the mysterious Rhode, who was supposedly Seth's aunt. He walked toward the stairs. His big black boots with the hardened wooden heels that protected him from flying embers and molten glass clacked out loudly on the floor. Mary Jane recovered quickly from her accidental near-fall, and she clambered back up the stairs again where she couldn't be seen. Jake called out to his daughter in such a way that she knew that he meant what he said. But she also knew he wasn't really mad at her.

"What, Father?" Mary Jane called out in a voice slightly over a whisper in an attempt to deceive her father into believing that she was battling to keep her crystal blue eyes open. It didn't work.

"Mary Jane, don't make me count to ten before I come up

and make you get into bed." Mary Jane shook with revulsion at those words. Jake Bell knew that the way to show his daughter that he really meant what he said was to treat her like a child. She hated it, and he knew it so very well. True, Mary Jane was really still a child. But, she had been the woman of the Bell house for so long that she considered herself to be almost grown up. So it particularly galled her when her father made her feel so childish. It was his way of saying, "Mary Jane, get to bed. I mean it!"

"Oh, Father. Okay!" Mary Jane conceded, and she bounced up the stairs and into her loft bedroom. Mary Jane figured she probably could make out most everything they said anyway, so she went ahead and got into bed. Mary Jane made sure that the trundle beds legs scraped on the floor when she got into the warm, comfortable sleeping "manger" so that her father would know she had obeyed him.

It worked. As soon as Jake Bell heard the bed scrape on the loft floor, his hefty boots announced with each echoing step that he was rejoining his white-haired visitor.

Mary Jane listened closely to the whispering voices. She didn't dare to get out of the trundle bed to go back to the top of the stairs, because her keen-eared father would hear her, and then she would most assuredly catch it. So Mary Jane resigned herself to straining as hard as she could to hear the now almost inaudible voices.

Mary Jane imagined that she could make out a few words of her father and Rhode's conversation as she struggled to stay awake. But much to her chagrin, she could hear Jake and Rhode stroll into the glassblowing workshop, and the words became just a mumbled and garbled blur.

As she couldn't make anything from their conversation, Mary Jane gave up and decided to change for bed. Without making a sound or leaving bed, she removed her clothing and placed them carefully in the small cedar chest at the foot of the bed. Then she pulled her warm flannel nightgown from the cedar chest and slowly tugged it on. The gray flannel bed shirt was plain, but Mary Jane was so thankful that it was warm and comforting. On this night, she liked the calming reassurance that her old flannel nightdress gave her. After she finally settled into her small bed, Mary Jane struggled to stay awake. She could still hear that Rhode and her father were deep in serious conversation, and she wanted to stay awake in case they came back into the sitting room right below her loft. But Mary Jane was exhausted; it had been a very long day and . . . night. She finally pulled up the warm blankets to her nose and then tumbled into a very deep but restless sleep.

CHAPTER 5

THE WEEK WOULD pass quickly for Seth and Andrew, but not for Mary Jane. Saturday night seemed to come around about the way most kids think Christmas comes around: slowly. This described Mary Jane's week exactly. Even though she had been told by her father to stick close to the house, Mary Jane was determined to be at the Old Glory Holiness Church to hear what Katherine had to say on Saturday. The episode with Rhode only made her more curious. When she awoke the next day, she quizzed her father about the woman. Unable to get a straight answer, Mary Jane decided to wait a few days.

"What did Rhode want to talk with you about?" Mary Jane said nonchalantly Thursday night as she washed the evening dinner dishes.

"Nothing important," Jake said. But Mary Jane knew her father well, and she knew that something was wrong from the look on his face. He was troubled, very deeply troubled. He had acted like this all week, deep worry lines etching his handsome face. When he was worried, her father also had the habit of chewing on his lower lip. That week Jake Bell almost brought his bottom lip to blood, he chewed on it so incessantly. Mary Jane did get the dishes done, but got no answer from her father. She finally dropped the subject. But Mary Jane's blue eyes flashed with determination and curiosity. She decided that come Saturday night, she was going to be at the meeting, or drama club, or class, or preaching, or lecture, or confessional, or teaching . . . whatever Katherine was presenting to them. Mary Jane was determined to be there, regardless of what her father said. She was going to get to the bottom of all this whispering and gossip, or at least she was going to learn as much as she could.

That week, Katherine talked to her students only about reading, writing and arithmetic. The dark-tressed teacher didn't say anything to her three special pupils about their upcoming meeting. Mary Jane could tell, or perhaps it is better said she knew, that Katherine was going to be there, and that something was going to happen. Mary Jane instinctively felt that something was amiss in her life, or perhaps in the community. Anyway and somehow, it included her and her father.

"Seth, promise me you're going to be there Saturday night!" Mary Jane asked, almost begging, after school on Friday.

Seth had a scared look on his face. He said he was going to be there. If the truth be known, if it wasn't for Mary Jane's presence, Seth wouldn't be there at all. Andrew was a different story. Mary Jane thought he would be scared as she and Seth were.

"I wouldn't miss it for the world," Andrew bragged, with not one ounce of fear or concern in his voice.

"Aw, you probably know that you can't even be there 'cause your parents won't let you out of their sight."

"What's going on?" came a nosy, high-pitched voice behind them. Maggie had seen the threesome speaking and had slowly walked up behind them.

"Nothing, Maggie," Andrew exclaimed, trying to ignore the young blonde.

"What's going on Saturday night?" Maggie asked, realizing that she had overheard something that maybe she shouldn't have. She was dying to know what was going on.

"Maggie, I swear to you that nothing is going on."

"If you don't tell me about it, I will tell my pappy," Maggie bragged, daring the threesome to exclude her now. "He's the most stubborn man in these here mountains; he'll want to find out what is going on." Though Maggie was very young, she was smart, and she was right about her father, the Reverend Cane. If something was happening in the community, no one knew how but he found out things that other people had not told a soul. Mary Jane, Seth and Andrew rolled their eyes at each other.

Finally, Mary Jane decided they better let Maggie in on their secret.

"No, don't tell Maggie," Seth pleaded. "She'll tell her father for sure."

"No, I will not!" Maggie said dramatically. "But if you don't tell me, I will for sure tell my pappy."

Seth sighed, "Well, all right, it's no big deal. You weren't at the last meeting anyway."

"You're going to have another secret meeting with teacher?" Maggie exclaimed excitedly.

"Yes, we are, Maggie," Mary Jane said. Then Seth and Andrew tried to keep Mary Jane quiet, but she continued. "And you are invited—it wasn't the same without you there, Maggie. Please do come, please," Mary Jane said in her most earnest voice.

"I don't even know that I would want to come to your dumb old club anyway," Maggie said, a big frown coming to her face. "My pappy heard about your meeting, and he said it would be a waste of time for some old drama club about Sheekspeare."

"That's Shakespeare," Andrew corrected the youngster.

"That's what I said!" Maggie interjected. "My pappy said studying that rubbish was a waste of time. The Reverend Cane said that the only literature I needed to learn was the Good Book." With that pronouncement Maggie turned on her heel and went stomping off.

"How did you know that would work, Mary Jane?" Seth asked, obviously impressed.

"Never underestimate the power of a woman's intuition," Mary Jane said proudly. Neither Andrew, Mary Jane or Seth, or even the little one, Maggie, said another word about Saturday night. Maggie seemed to be unconcerned about the drama club and didn't bring it up again. Even when school let out Friday afternoon, the threesome didn't mention Saturday night. Mary Jane suspected she might be the only one there, but so be it, she thought, so be it. Mary Jane was determined she would be there, come Hell or high water.

Saturday arrived cold and windy, although the wind slowly died down later that afternoon. A blanket of freezing smoke settled in over the mountains. Good, Mary Jane thought, the better to camouflage her leaving the Bell house. Mary Jane stayed away from her father all day, then right before twilight was beginning to cloak the mountains, she yelled out to her father, "Be back in a jiffy, Father. I'm going to the Reagan's store to get something." Jake Bell was so intent in his workshop that he never looked up as Mary Jane slid out the front door, undetected, she thought.

Mary Jane was the first of the three students to show up at the meeting. Seth, Andrew and Mary Jane had never really come up with a definitive way to describe their little group get-together. The rickety Old Glory Holiness Church, by the

Old River Cemetery, was a favorite meeting spot of mischievous boys. Its weather-beaten clapboard hadn't been painted in years. Mary Jane couldn't understand why Miss Katherine would choose this place for their meeting, but it did have a stage. A perfect place to re-enact this legend.

As soon as Mary Jane arrived, she was surprised to see how spooky the place looked. Its haunted appearance made her swallow hard, but she had declared that she was going to be there whether Seth or Andrew showed up, so she bolstered her courage and walked on up to the crumbling old church house.

The cemetery of the Old Glory Holiness Church had been kept up for a while by some of the old families who had relatives buried there. But most of the families had died or moved out of the mountains when the U.S. government confiscated their land for the national park. The abandoned building and lot had slowly become a mess. Old tangled vines and grown-up thickets of brambles surrounded the place. Still, this was where the group had decided to hold their club meeting, and Katherine was going to begin their lessons by telling the story of Tennessee's most famous folk tale, the legend of the Bell Witch.

At one time, some gypsies had inhabited the old church, but they had been chased out of town. Since then the church sat by itself alone, slowly deteriorating. The outside was weather-worn, and parts of the steeple were beginning to fall off. The church needed major repair, but it was not to be.

Other than the dilapidated appearance, the old church was a perfect place for a presentation, dramatization or class. There was an elevated stage where the minister and choir had sat facing the congregation. It was perfect for the youngsters to discuss issues, hold a drama club or tell a ghost story. The inside was built like a little theater, and the acoustics were perfect for a presentation or a one-woman play.

Someone had placed candles everywhere and left long-stemmed matches. Mary Jane began to light the candles. Soon a soft glow emanated from the myriad candles, and it gave the once-forbidding rectory a nice hue. As soon as Mary Jane lighted the candles she saw a pile of wood stacked neatly in the huge stone fireplace. Tonight was not as cold as it had been recently—surely not nearly as cold as the first night they met and persuaded Miss Katherine to tell her rendition of the Bell Witch story. Mary Jane was reluctant at first to start a fire in such an old fireplace. Surely it was a fire hazard. Still, she pulled her long blonde hair to one side so as not to allow any nasty soot to get on her hair. Taking special care to protect the brown combs that had once held her mother's hair in place, she threw open the damper and peered up into the clear, cold Smoky Mountain air. She could see stars twinkling above. If the chimney is this clear, Mary Jane reasoned, I don't see how starting a fire could harm anything. It was truly cold in the old building, but soon a roaring fire was burning in the big fireplace.

"Where is everyone?" Mary Jane whispered as she hugged herself in front of the blazing oak logs now crackling and popping in the stone fireplace. "It would be just like everyone but me to chicken out on this, because this is the most boring town in America," she said. Mary Jane then went back to the task of lighting the rest of the candles.

Seth and Andrew both burst through the front doors laughing and knocked over some of the candles.

"Watch it, boys," Mary Jane exclaimed.

"I hope that little Maggie is reading the Good Book like her father wants her to," Seth said, as he helped Mary Jane attach the candles to the floor with drops of wax.

"Yeah," John said. "She is such a little pest."

"I hate to say it," Mary Jane said, "but I will have to say I agree with you. But she's not going to show up, I promise you. Especially after the way I begged her to please, please, come," Mary Jane said. All three laughed out loud at tricking the pixieish blonde. They considered her too immature for the group, anyway, even though the three children weren't but three or four years older than Maggie. But when one is their age, three or four years seems to be a lot.

"I doubt that Reverend Cane would let his beloved daughter come to this desolate place to hear a ghost story," Seth added.

"Forget her," Andrew said. "I can't wait for this show to get started!" Mary Jane couldn't believe the confident manner that Andrew displayed. This scary old church still made her nervous, and she knew Seth was twitchy, too. But she couldn't help but admire Andrew—he truly did seem eager to hear this story Katherine was going to tell. The three of them looked at each other in the dim light. Although the fireplace was now blazing, the interior of the church was still dark and daunting. All of a sudden, their plans of holding a class meeting here seemed, in a word, silly. And, to be more accurate, scary. It was just the three of them, after all, and although Miss Katherine was a nice lady, no one really knew that much about her. Where did she come from? How did she become such an expert on the Bell Witch?

The three youngsters did what generations of youngsters did when they discovered that an idea they had cooked up suddenly didn't seem to be such a good idea: They started to talk themselves into it again. "We're going to learn from it just like other students have learned from the way Shakespeare took legends and myths and made great works of literature," Seth declared as he walked over to the fireplace to warm his hands.

"You're probably right; I hear the Bell Witch story is a good scary one," Andrew joined in. But if Andrew was scared, he wasn't showing it.

"I say the scarier the better," Mary Jane piped in, trying to build her own confidence as she began to light more candles. "From Shakespeare's 'The Tempest' to Edgar Allen Poe's 'The Pit and the Pendulum,' ghost stories and legends have encouraged great literature."

"Durn, me lady, you are set on gaining knowledge from the literary masters of the ages," Seth said, turning his back on the fire and bowing deeply to Mary Jane. He turned back to Andrew and they both raised their eyebrows, not in making fun of her, exactly, but of the way that Mary Jane was able to express her knowledge of the great writers. Both Seth and Andrew knew that this girl was pretty, but they also knew she was pretty smart. And to Seth, this made her that much more attractive.

"We'll, let's get started then," came a voice behind them. Katherine had pushed through the front doors so quietly that the three children had not noticed her come in. She stood before them, her long, raven hair loose on her shoulders. She wore a dark cape that covered her from head to toe. The pointed hood added an eerie accent to the mysterious teacher. The robe draped to the floor and when she walked, it was almost if she glided over the old wooden floor.

Seth, Andrew and Mary Jane sat there with their mouths gaping, not really knowing what to think of their teacher. She was quiet and almost shy at school. True, Katherine had shown a side of her that they had not seen before when she spoke of Rhode at their last get-together. But now Seth, Andrew and Mary Jane couldn't believe their eyes. Now, she had taken on some kind of other-worldly appearance. They couldn't have been more shocked.

Mary Jane had the common sense to continue lighting candles to hide her uncertainty. This was Mary Jane's idea, more or less, but now that the time was here, she had no idea what was going to take place. Katherine, it seemed, knew exactly what was going to happen. The slight teacher with dark, dark hair approached the stage at the front of the old church. She walked to an old wooden pulpit off to the side of the stage.

As Andrew, Seth and Mary Jane feigned being busy, they secretly watched Katherine lug the pulpit to the center of the stage. When Katherine was certain that she had the podium right at the center of the stage, she slowly lowered her hood, then took off the cape. The kids' minds were set somewhat at ease now that the flickering lights revealed the teacher they knew at school.

"So how do we start?" Mary Jane finally got the courage to ask as she straightened up from lighting the very last candle.

"We just get started," Katherine said as she stood behind the broken-down pulpit. "But I need an audience or congregation," Katherine said as she waved for the trio to be seated.

Seth, John and Mary Jane piled into the first pew right in front of their teacher. "Tell it from the start," Seth exhorted, as he and Andrew jostled to make sure Mary Jane sat in between them.

"There's only one way to tell a story, my daddy says, and that's straight from the beginning," Andrew said.

Mary Jane smiled and looked up at the raven-haired lady. "I've always heard of this legend, but I never heard it from the very start to finish."

Katherine nodded her head in acknowledgment. "You're right, children!" Katherine said as she paced back and forth. "There is no place to start except at the beginning.

"I was going to tell you all about my history, but I believe now that is not the right way to do this. I believe it is best to tell of the things that started at first," she said.

"You see it all began in 1817 in Adams, Tennessee, a small hamlet outside of Nashville. I'm going to tell you the story the way I heard it, as I know it, just as if we all had been there ourselves to hear the whole, terrible, unbelievable story of the Bell Witch." With that, Katherine looked upward at the rafters.

Seth, Mary Jane and Andrew sat in rapt attention as their teacher pulled her far-away gaze back to the children. Her bright eyes glazed over, and Katherine cleared her throat. Then she looked out over the dilapidated old church house as if she were going to give a performance in Carnegie Hall. Katherine raised both arms to the ceiling and then slowly allowed them to drop to her side. Then she looked from Seth to Andrew and then finally to Mary Jane. Katherine began to speak in a slow, rhythmic voice.

CHAPTER **6**

"YOU KNOW, JOHN Bell left the state of North Carolina when he really wasn't much older than you, Seth and Andrew," Katherine said, looking down from her pulpit at the two boys where they sat on either side of Mary Jane. The teacher continued, "John Bell was looking for a way to make a living, to support his farm and his lovely bride Lucy. Perhaps you, Seth and Andrew, have thought of a way to make a living so that you could ask Mary Jane to marry you," she said.

That comment brought a snicker of embarrassment from all three. Mary Jane held up her hand. "What is it, Mary Jane?" Katherine asked.

"Miss Katherine, I thought you said this was the story of the Bell Witch." The thin schoolteacher sensed the point of Mary Jane's question, that this comment was not really relevant to the story. Katherine smiled a bit and responded with a nod of her head.

"You're right, Mary Jane; this is the story of the Bell Witch. I thought the reference to you, Seth and Andrew would add some pertinence to the situation, but you have made a valid point, my dear. I will continue."

Katherine raised her thin, fragile hands to the ceiling and continued, trying to keep to the story. "John Bell was a very industrious man. It was not long before he had done very well for himself in the small town of Adams. Oh yes, John Bell had it all: a beautiful wife, Lucy, who loved him dearly. A lush green farm that was spread out over the rich farm country. Three healthy, loving and lovely children. Success, by any person's definition in the 1800s, was John Bell's. Some might say he had it too good. Neighbors wondered, 'How did John Bell get so well off so quickly?'"

"The years passed. Soon, his oldest son, John Bell Jr., went off to fight alongside General Andrew Jackson. And that, my three young students," Katherine stated as she dropped her hands to her sides, "is where we start our story. The following narrative is the account, the true account, mind you, of what happened." Katherine solemnly looked at the three members of the ragtag drama club. "I am now going to relay to you the crux of our story," she said. "There were all sorts of rumors that have gone around about this story, but this is it; this is what really happened!"

Katherine flashed a big smile and restarted her story.

"You see, the whole town of Adams was having a big celebration on John Bell's farm. There was a huge bonfire, children were running around and playing. The whole town had smiles on their faces. John Bell and his wife Lucy were talking to one another as they watched the town folks have a good time. . . ."

"It's a real nice turnout, John," Lucy Bell said while hugging her loving husband. "It is, isn't it. It's even a bigger turnout than last year, I suppose," he replied.

"Look at Betsy, John," Lucy sighed. "This might be the last celebration we have as a family together. Betsy's growing up so fast. You know, she's gonna be a woman soon, and she already has to beat the boys off with a tree branch."

Sixteen-year-old Betsy Bell was gathered with her best

friends, Theny Thorne and Joshua Gardner, both seventeen. "Dance with me, Betsy," Joshua asked as he swept her off her feet and into a whirling square dance that had formed in the field. With a mother's loving eye, Lucy watched the happy couple, "A few years ago, she would have been bobbing for apples. Now, she's only interested in that Joshua. I think she falling in love with that boy."

"Gardner's a good boy. He's a good farmer, too," John replied, also noticing the sparkle in his daughter's eye.

"Look over there, John," Lucy nudged her husband, nodding toward an older lady laughing with other guests. "There's old Kate Batts; she showed up."

John eyed the cantankerous old woman, "To tell you the truth, I could not have cared less if she had showed up."

"She's been so cranky; it's nice to see her smiling for once." Lucy added, trying to make sure her husband remained peaceable and friendly to all their guests that day.

John squinted, "Is that the schoolteacher she's talking to? My old eyes don't see too well at night."

"I believe it is, John," his wife replied.

John scowled a bit. "There's just something about him that doesn't sit well with me."

"What do you mean, John?"

"We'll he's nice enough and everything, and educated, but there is something behind those eyes that I disagree with. I don't know what it is. What does he do when he goes up North on those trips of his? No one I know needs to travel up North as often as that man does."

Lucy Bell looked at her husband, "John Bell, stop it right now. That teacher is a good man. He has taught our children well."

"Well hello there, Mrs. Lucy Bell. How are you this evening?" James Johnston implored of his hostess.

"Just fine. And how about yourself, Mr. James Johnston? How are you?"

"Couldn't be finer, Mrs. Bell." James Johnston was one of the Bell's dearest friends. A tall handsome man of about forty, James's hard work and helpfulness made him well-liked in Adams.

James thrust his hand towards his dear friend, "John. Good to see you."

"It's good to see you too, James. I understand you just bought yourself a right smart bit of land."

"That's right," James Johnston proudly confirmed. "Ten acres."

Always neighborly, John offered, "If you need a hand in getting it going, just let me know."

James Johnston nodded his head in appreciation. "That's kind of you John, but you're too busy to be helping me. You've got your own farm to tend to, not to mention you've got your hands full with those three kids of yours."

John Bell laughed slightly in agreement. "They are a handful. Lucy and I were just talking about them. Betsy's all grown up now, and paying all her attention to boys. Heck, John Junior just returned from the war a little while back. He fought under General Jackson. Then there's Williams. Now he's a handful. Always running around, getting into trouble. He's the one we have to keep our eye on."

Later that evening, as the shade of darkness obscured everyone and everything, Betsy Bell met Joshua Gardner behind the family barn. She and Joshua were holding hands. After looking around to make sure no one was watching them, they began to kiss. Joshua pulled away breathlessly and said in a lowered whisper, "I love you, Betsy Bell."

"Please don't say that Joshua," Betsy begged, batting her big eyes up at Joshua.

"Why can't I say it, Betsy? I mean it."

"It embarrasses me," Betsy replied. "It's the truth," Joshua said.

"Joshua, we need to get back to the celebration before anyone sees we are gone."

"Betsy, who cares if they know?" Joshua asked, his eyes probing hers.

"I just don't want my parents to come looking for us." "You're right; this isn't proper. I need to speak to your parents anyway," Joshua said as he pulled Betsy to him by her waist and kissed her hard.

Back at the party, everyone had gathered around the Bell house. Professor Powell and John Bell were engaged in deep conversation, drinking glasses of fruit juice made right there on the Bell farm. Both men smiled slightly while watching the throng sing and dance.

"John, it's a very nice party."

"Thanks, Professor," John said as he raised his glass in a slight salute. "Is Williams staying out of trouble at school? We've been having some trouble with him recently."

"No John, Williams is doing fine. He just needs to focus a bit more on his schoolwork," the Professor reassured John, patting him softly on the shoulder.

"Well, if you have any problem with Williams, you just let me know. I'll straighten him out."

The dark night shadows hid a lot of the revelry, but the men still spied the outlines of two young people walking up from behind the barn. The Professor took special notice of the couple and commented on the young woman approaching.

"John, your daughter, Betsy, is one of my best pupils."

"Yeah, Betsy is a good girl," her father responded.

"She's growing up fast, John. She's going to make some man a fine wife some day."

John Bell looked over at Professor Powell, who continued to stare at Betsy.

"You wouldn't think that husband would be you, Professor?" John asked a little sharply.

"I was just joking around, John. Of course, anyone can see that Betsy is still just a child," the Professor said.

"Many a truth is said in jest, Professor. Excuse me."

"Yes, it is was nice talking with you, Mr. Bell," he said as John Bell walked away. Bidding his adieu, he walked away into the night.

He walked directly past Lucy, who was sitting with two of her friends, chatting and knitting socks. She barely noticed the Professor brush her hair with the back of his hand as he passed. Her attention was focused on the approaching Kate Batts, who barreled toward the groups as if on a mission. Thinking quickly, Lucy said, "Hide your pins everyone, here comes old Kate Batts."

The women quickly hid the pins that were holding up parts of their outfits. Old Kate Batts—who was in her late sixties but said she was forty-nine—approached the trio of women.

"Hello, ya'll," Kate said happily. "Hello, Kate," the group responded in kind.

"I was just on my way home for the day and thought I'd stop and say goodbye."

Lucy Bell looked up from her knitting and asked, "Kate, you leaving already?"

"Yes, I am not as young as I used to be, and I do need my beauty sleep, you know," Kate said without blushing. "Before I leave you, may I ask if any of you kind ladies have any extra pins I could have?"

Without breaking a smile, the group continued their knitting and answered in unison, "No, not even one."

Kate tittered and said, "Well, that's okay, ladies. Lucy,

is your husband around? I would like to talk to him before I leave."

Lucy looked up from her knitting and pointed to her husband, "Kate, he is directly over there. Standing next to Mr. Johnston." Kate nodded in appreciation. "Good night, ladies." She headed toward John Bell. The group suppressed its laughter until Lucy burst out, "She is getting crazy in her old age. What does she want all of those pins for?" A roar of laughter peeled from the other ladies—each trying to be as polite and Christian about the situation as possible.

Kate walked up to the barn where John Bell was talking with a neighbor.

"I need to talk with you, Bell," Kate interrupted without saying "excuse me" or anything. "How do you do, Mrs. Batts?" John replied while turning slowly to face her.

"Bell, we haven't yet settled our business transaction." "Well Mrs. Batts, you're mistaken," he replied. "I settled that with your husband just last week."

"Don't talk to me as if I know nothing, Mr. Bell. My husband doesn't handle any business affairs; he wouldn't know what to do. Don't think that because I am a woman that you can cheat me on a land deal and I wouldn't find out."

John took a deep breath. "Mrs. Batts, your husband is fully competent to handle such affairs. If you are not happy with the transaction, I suggest you take it up with your husband."

"All right, then. But we're not finished yet. You haven't heard the end of this, John Bell." Mrs. Batts walked off in a huff.

To no one in particular, John Bell responded, "I am sure I haven't."

A few moments later, the preacher from the Bell's church arrived at the celebration. He carried a big basket of fruit as he walked up to Lucy.

"Hello, Mrs. Lucy," the preacher man said, as handed her the basket of fruit. The preacher walked over to where John Bell Senior was talking with his namesake.

"Reverend," John Senior extended his hand to the preacher. "How are you?"

As the two shook hands, the preacher replied, "God has created a wonderful evening for a celebration." "That he has, Reverend," John Senior said, waving his hand toward the evening sky in a grand gesture. Then, spotting the tall, muscular young man approaching them, John said, "You remember my son, John Junior, don't you, Reverend?"

Junior and the preacher shook hands and smiled at each other.

"Yes, but I haven't seen you around in a long time young man."

"How do you do, sir?" Junior asked the Reverend.

John Bell happily informed the Reverend, "Did you know that my son was off fighting for General Andrew Jackson during the Battle of New Orleans?"

"No I didn't, John. Is that so?" the preacher asked. John Junior proudly added, "Yes sir, it's true. I just got home to Adams a few days ago."

"We're glad to have you home, son," the preacher said as he shook Junior's hand again.

"And I will tell you, Reverend; it is good to be home again."

"Well how is ol' Andy Jackson, son? What's he like?"

"He's a great general," the boy replied. "Taught us everything we know. He thinks he can beat anybody in battle."

"I bet old Andy could, too," the Preacher responded proudly.

"We do have a great Army, sir. And most of it is because of General Jackson."

As Junior regaled the Reverend with tales of Old Hickory, Joshua Gardner took his opportunity to speak privately with John Bell. Joshua nervously asked, "May I speak to you, Mr. Bell?"

"What can I do for you, Joshua?" "Well, Mr. Bell, sir, I . . . " Joshua stammered nervously, as he alternately twisted his cap in his hand and used it to wipe his sweating brow.

"I was wondering, Mr. Bell, sir," Joshua continued, trying to work up the courage to speak, "if it would be okay with you . . . if I were to ask your daughter's hand in marriage?"

John Bell looked down at the very nervous young man. "Joshua, does she want to marry you?"

"Well, Mr. Bell, sir, I'm not exactly sure." Joshua responded, his voice cracking.

"Well, Joshua, you better find that out first, don't you think?" With a fatherly wink, John Bell blessed their young love.

"Amazing Grace, how sweet the sound, lah-dum de dum de dum. . . ." Lucy Bell's voice trailed as she dug in the earth. The day was crystalline without a cloud in the sky. John had just returned from his meeting. He bounded towards the porch and his beloved wife.

Unable to keep from cracking the biggest smile, Lucy called out, "Do I even have to ask?"

"He wants to buy as much as he can!" John exclaimed, finally reaching the porch steps before plopping down, out of breath.

"That's wonderful news!" Lucy dropped her trowel to hug her husband.

"It is great news, Lucy," John replied. "I just hope we can produce enough wheat for him. It's been a difficult spring for growing." John looked around the place and asked, "Where's the kids?"

"Well, Betsy's over at Theny's house and the boys are out working in the field." John looked out across his farm. "They better not be messing around that cave."

Lucy replied, "I told the boys they weren't allowed around the cave, that it would upset you. Speaking of upsets, have you talked to Kate Batts since yesterday?"

John shook his head. "I have not."

"Rumor going around the women is that if you two don't settle this soon, she will go to the church with her grievance," Lucy sighed.

"Let her go, then." John said without blinking an eye. "I settled all of this a week ago with Mr. Batts."

Lucy nodded her head. "Well, John, I hope you are right."

"What are you planting in the yard?" he asked his wife.

"Some vines, John. They're going to make the house look real nice one day."

John laughed. "Darling, you are going to get us covered up in those vines."

Later that afternoon, down in the field, the Bell boys, Junior and Williams, were hard at work. The young men weren't having much luck clearing a large tree trunk from the middle of the field. They tied a rope around the stubborn trunk and attached the other end to an even more stubborn root. Williams dug rapidly at the rock-laden soil among the roots.

"Have you got it dug up yet, Williams?" Junior hollered back from his position atop Kim, the tough plough horse.

Williams wiped the sweat from his brow and after one more heave with the shovel said, "Almost."

Williams dug a bit more, shoveling dirt from around the roots. Finally, he shouted at his brother, "Okay, Junior." With a wave of his hand, he yelled, "Go ahead and pull."

Junior dug his heels into the ribs of his horse, and Kim started to pull. Williams leaned on the tree stump and pushed as hard as he could. Williams's muscles bulged and his veins and eyes popped. Junior's horse was kicking dirt high into the air as it strained against the weight of the huge trunk. The horse snorted and dug in again. Slowly but surely the stump began to stir as the trunk slowly moved away from its earthen embrace.

"Keep pushing, brother; we almost got it."

Inch by inch, the trunk and attached stump began to stir until the stump finally emerged from its hole, with red clay clinging to every small root.

"Whoa," Williams yelled as he disappeared beneath the liberated stump. He tried to grab hold of something, but the Earth just seemed to swallow him up. Unbeknownst to the Bell boys, a huge cave lay beneath the farm, and lo and behold, Williams fell in.

John Junior jumped off the horse and ran to the edge of the hole, barely able to keep from sliding over the edge himself.

Down below, Williams slowly got up, testing each limb in turn. He discovered he hadn't broken anything, dusted himself off and stared up at the shaft of light that streamed down into the cave from over his head.

"Williams, Williams, are you okay?" came a shout from Junior.

Williams, still in shock from his quick descent, peered up at his brother and yelled, "Yeah, yeah, I'm all right, I think." He looked around at the darkness surrounding him. "Get me out of here, John Junior!"

"Hang on, brother; I'm coming!"

Williams, reassured that rescue was coming, started poking around in the near-darkness. Exploring mostly with his hands, he came upon something soft but heavy. Curious, he drug it over to the shaft of light, barely noticing the strange odor his bundle emitted.

One more tug and Williams got the first glimpse of his cave treasure. The stench now filled Williams's nostrils and he understood that the heavy, loamy object he lugged was a dead body.

"AHH . . . AHH . . ." Williams's scream echoed throughout the cave. He wanted to run, but was afraid to leave the light. Suddenly something grabbed him.

"AHHH . . . AHHHH . . . " he screamed again.

"It's me, Williams, it's me, Junior." He had joined his brother in the cave by using the rope from the tree trunk. Breath heaving from the shock, Williams's terror turned to wonderment. "Look at this, Junior," Williams finally gasped out, pulling on Junior's arm.

"Look at this, Junior," he insisted. "What it is?" John Junior asked. He couldn't see much in the dark, and he couldn't make out what his brother had found.

"It's a body, brother; it's a body. It's a dead person."

Junior leaned over once more, letting the light fall on the lump at his feet. "Good grief, it's stuck full of pins." The glimmer of at least twenty pins of different shapes and sizes poked out of the mummified mass.

"Why are all those pins stuck into it like that?"

John Junior said, "I don't know."

Williams bent to remove one of the pins. Junior screamed, "What are you doing?! Williams, don't touch it."

"I want to look at them in the daylight. They might be worth something." He slowly and carefully removed the pins from the body, placing them in a satchel attached to his belt.

"I'm warning you, Williams. If dad finds out about this, you are going to get a whipping."

"You aren't going to tell Father?" Williams pleaded.

"No, but I'm warning you, brother, you could get into a heap of trouble, and I mean it."

John Junior shook his head in disgust. "Let's get out of here."

Williams called out, "I'm right behind you."

The two brothers grabbed on to the rope and began to pull themselves out of the cave, hand over hand. Their combined weight put too much stress on the rope. As it snapped, the duo were sent tumbling back into the dark cave. They stood up and stared at the small point of light high above their heads.

"I'm scared," Williams whispered.

"Don't worry. We'll get out of here," Junior said in a voice that was meant to be reassuring, but was not.

"Look, Williams," John Junior said excitedly, "There is an exit out of here. Look." John Junior pulled Williams along with him. "Look, Williams, this must lead out of here." Junior pulled on Williams harder. "This must be a way out."

"I'm afraid. I think we should wait for someone to come and get us out of here," Williams said reluctantly.

"You big sissy," Junior exclaimed at his brother's weakness. "I'm going to find a way out; you can stay here if you want to, Williams. " Junior let go of Williams and took off exploring, searching for a way out of their predicament. "I'm getting out of here."

"Don't lose me in this place!" Williams pleaded as he struggled along with his brother, sliding around the cave floor.

John Junior struggled along, too, trying to keep his footing. He bravely yelled out, "Just hang on to me."

Half-climbing, half-crawling, they scrambled up a slight hill into a different chamber in the cave.

"Williams, look over there!" John Junior exclaimed as they saw a small pinpoint of light. Struggling forward, they emerged from the cavern. After the dimness, they both had to shield their eyes against the light exploding brilliantly in all directions.

Still shading his offended eyes, John Junior reached over and punched Williams playfully on the arm.

"Yahoo!!!!" The whoops of glee filled the open sky as loudly as two lungs could. "See Williams, I told you so, I told you I'd find us a way out. Ol' Hickory Jackson couldn't have done a better job of leading the men out of trouble than I did, if I do say so myself."

"Good grief," Williams whispered to himself, "now he is comparing himself to Andrew Jackson." After liberating themselves from their dark prison, the boys' courage returned. Forgetting the horror of their subterranean imprisonment, they decided to return to the cavern. They stumbled around looking for the way back.

"Here it is," Williams declared as he kicked some earth away from the hole. Then Williams and Junior peered deep into the darkened chasm.

"Where is it?" They looked at each other, gauging whether the other had spotted the body. Both shook their heads. There was no body.

"Where'd it go?" Williams asked his brother as he continued to look frantically around. "Who knows, Williams?" John Junior laughed, "Maybe the old boy got cold and decided to leave," he teased his young brother. Williams stopped searching the dark opening and looked at his brother.

"That's not funny, John Junior."

CHAPTER **7**

"BOYS! LUNCHTIME! COME and get it," came the sweet voice of their mother drifting over the field, calling Williams and John Junior home for their noon-day meal. They looked at each other again and then turned around and made a mad dash toward the house. Williams held tightly onto the satchel full of pins. Clumsily, he tripped over a dirt clod and fell sprawling, face first. The pins flew everywhere over the ground. Down on all fours, Williams frantically scrambled to reclaim his loot.

"Help me, Brother," Williams pleaded.

"You're going to lose our treasure after only a few minutes," Junior mocked, but then came to the rescue and joined Williams in the search.

Williams retorted, "I am not going to lose anything." The brothers quickly picked up the pins and raced on towards the house. But one pin escaped the young treasure hunters. The lone bejeweled pin glistened brilliantly in the sun, as if beckoning another to pick it up and claim it for their own.

"Joshua, why are you so fidgety?" Betsy Bell inquired later that day in the Bell woods, as she and Joshua leaned against a tree. The boy was obviously antsy—he was picking stones off the forest floor and chucking them at a tree trunk several yards away. Joshua picked up one last stone and threw it particularly hard, making it ricochet wildly away.

He turned to Betsy.

"I got something to say to you, Betsy. Something to ask really. Something I've been wanting to ask for some time now."

Betsy leaned against the tree, her young beauty radiating in the late afternoon light. "What is it, Joshua Gardner?" Betsy teased.

Joshua stammered around some. "Betsy, well, we've been spending a lot of time together. And I love you . . . and I think that you love me. Shortly here, I'll be all finished with school. I was just wondering . . . it would make me a very happy man . . . well, I was wondering if you would marry me?"

Betsy pushed herself away from the trunk and turned from Joshua.

Joshua stammered to her back. "My father's already given me a small cabin, and I'll make enough money to support a family," he explained.

"It's not that, Joshua," she said without turning around. "I love you, I do. I know you'd be a terrific husband and father and we'd be happy." Betsy turned and took a step toward Joshua. "It's just that I am not ready to get married. We're still young. I don't want to have children yet. I don't want to move away from my family yet. I fancy you, and maybe one day we will get married, but just not right now."

Joshua didn't say anything but shook his head in frustration and threw one last stone as far away as he could, which sent it cascading into the canopy of green leaves that stretched out in front of him. A hurt look descended over Joshua's face. The sting from Betsy's words planted deeply into his heart.

Resolved, Joshua took his beloved's hand gently and lovingly said, "Betsy, I will give you this summer to finish out your childhood and will ask you once again next harvest. Maybe then you will be ready."

"Well, Joshua, you're still going to have to ask my parents first."

Pulling Betsy close, Joshua brushed her hair aside. "Betsy, I already have." The couple kissed one last time before locking arms and slowly strolling from the privacy of the woods.

Dawn broke early and bright the following morning. In the fluorescent orange and red sky, a black bat dove in and out of the woods encircling the Bell farmhouse.

All in all, another beautiful day had begun in Adams. Williams went to school early, his glimmering pins tucked safely in his satchel. After taking a seat in the rear of the one-room schoolhouse, Williams spotted James Hawthorne. "Psst. James. James. Come here," Williams whispered to his good buddy. "Look what I found." Williams slipped the pins from his satchel. The bejeweled hat pins glittered in the morning light that shone through the paneled window. "I ain't never seen nothing like that before," James said. "Nothin' at all," came another voice. It was soft and feminine, the voice of Violet Jones. A chorus of awe began to emanate from the slowly growing crowd. Williams noticed the attention his treasure garnered and it made him feel proud. The admiration of his classmates continued as Williams excitedly told them all of the high adventure he and his brother had shared. "My brother and I found them in a cave," Williams explained to everyone. "I fell down in the cave and my brother helped me out. Anyway, it's the truth; I found all of these pins in the cave."

Unbeknownst to the children, who were wrapped up in Williams's tale, Professor Powell entered the schoolroom and slipped up behind the group, seeking the cause of the commotion.

"Good morning, children," the Professor said suddenly. Taken aback, the crowd of youngsters dispersed to their seats like a flushed covey of quail. Williams, half frightened out of his wits, dropped the pins on the floor, scattering them in many different directions like wooden pick-up sticks.

Professor Powell stood back a bit and admonished the school students: "Now all of you know, don't you, that there are to be no distractions when you come to school? You come here for an education. You are not here to play games."

Professor Powell coolly observed his students with a stern eye. "Isn't that right, youngsters?" he asked, re-emphasizing they knew the rules and should have been seated and studying quietly. Surveying all of the youngsters in the small room with a glinting eye, the Professor returned his attention to the Bell youngster. Spotting the pins lying along the floor of the school, Professor Powell's eyes opened wide. The thin teacher studied the pins intently, then asked, "Williams, what are those?" Williams bent to one knee and gently picked up all of the pins. "Williams, I am going to take these pins from you now, but you may retrieve them when school is out."

After taking the pins from Williams Bell, Professor Powell slowly surveyed the room. Walking as straight as a rail, he ran a bony hand through his greased-back hair before taking his place in front of the schoolroom. Quietly he placed the pins into his desk drawer.

The day seemed never-ending. The time between classes of arithmetic, spelling and writing crawled on and on.

Betsy eyed the remainder of the day's arithmetic lesson on the board: $8+5=13$. She was seated in the front of the classroom, a seat assigned by the Professor himself. She often saved the seat beside her for Joshua so they could chat quietly between lessons. But today's episode with Williams had the whole class on its best behavior. Unable to sit quietly any longer, Betsy wrote "I love you" on her black slate with chalk and slid it to Joshua. He read it. "I love you, too," he mouthed back. Professor Powell had watched the exchange from behind his book.

He had noticed Betsy's fetching pink dress from the moment she had entered the school building. The cut of the bodice made her look even more shapely than usual. He watched her lovely round bosom rise and fall with each breath. It was perfectly accentuated by a pink blush that draped from her collar bone underneath her frock. A blush that was put there by Joshua Gardner.

Professor Powell slowly slid one hand beneath his desktop and pulled open the top drawer. Allowing his eyes to drop from his prized student only once, the Professor removed a red bejeweled pin and slipped it into his book, *A Comparison of Standard Religion and the Occult*.

"Close your books; school is over for the day." The teacher cleared his throat as he surveyed the room of students as if they were his soldiers to command. Professor Powell stretched high on his long, lanky legs then stated eloquently, "You are all free. I will see you tomorrow when we will be mostly practicing simple arithmetic." The teacher waved his arm in a dismissive manner.

Then in a louder voice: "Williams Bell, I'd like for you to stop here at my desk on your way out."

Williams looked at Betsy, shrugged and sighed, then whispered, "I'll see you later." The boy shuffled toward his teacher's desk with slouched shoulders. The Professor sat down at his desk and pulled out the confiscated pins, "Young man, where did you find these?"

"Well sir, We . . . that is my brother, John Junior, and me . . . were digging up a tree stump in our field. We dug so deep that we opened up a cave, and we fell in. There were all of these pins there so we decided to take them with us. Professor, sir, I know it was wrong to take something that was valuable and wasn't mine, but I thought that they might be useful to someone or something," Williams explained, stuttering along. Not knowing what else to say, Williams stated bluntly, "So, Professor Powell, I decided to take them. . . ." Williams shrugged his shoulders and looked at his teacher sheepishly. "So I took them."

The Professor looked up at the obviously embarrassed Williams and said, "I don't want to see these again. There is no place for these at a schoolhouse. Do you understand me?"

Williams nodded his head in hearty agreement, glad that he had gotten by with just a reprimand.

"Oh, yes sir!" Williams responded, smiling widely.

"I will see you again tomorrow, Williams, and I trust that this won't happen again."

The hot Middle Tennessee day slowly turned into a comfortable Southern night. Lucy had prepared a big healthy dinner of meat, cornbread, rolls, vegetables and apple pies for the family. There was little conversation as everyone ate earnestly. Betsy finished first.

"May I be excused, Father?" she asked.

"Betsy, have you finished everything?" John Bell questioned his daughter as he searched her plate.

"Yes, sir, I have," Betsy replied.

"Okay, Betsy. You are excused," Mr. Bell said as he took the last piece of cornbread.

Williams tapped his foot nervously as Junior also excused himself. "Father, may I be excused?" Williams finally asked.

"Not just yet. We need to have a discussion," John said softly.

"What about, Father?" Williams stammered. He could feel the heat of trouble rising up his body.

"I'll help Junior gather some wood," Mother Lucy said, knowing that father and son needed some time alone. She slid her chair away from the dinner table and left the room. Williams wiggled in his chair, his foot tapping the floor in a disjointed staccato rhythm. The boy was petrified. If his father really was serious and wanted to talk with him, something was amiss and he knew it. After the hubbub at school today and the scolding he received from Professor Powell, Williams's heart began to beat more rapidly as he awaited his father's attention.

John Senior pushed his chair back and tapped the table with his left hand as he began to speak. "I had a talk with Professor Powell today when I ran into him in town. He mentioned a disturbance in class. Do you wish to tell me about it?"

Williams kept patting his foot; he couldn't help it, he was so nervous. "Well sir, the other day, Junior and I were clearing that big stump from the field and we fell into a cave. . . ."

John Senior cut in, "Son, I told you to stay out of that cave."

"It wasn't on purpose, Father. We didn't know it was there. I accidentally fell in and found this body."

John Senior got a disturbed look on his face, but let his son continue talking. "There were all sorts of fancy pins stuck into the body. I thought they might be worth something so I took them all. Today at the schoolhouse, Professor Powell caught me showing them off to some friends."

"Williams, do you still have those pins?" John Bell asked.

"Yes, sir."

"Let me see them," his father said sternly, holding out his hand.

Williams had his satchel by his foot underneath the table.

He opened it up and dropped the pins onto his father's outstretched hand. As John examined the pins, one cut his palm. "Ouch!" John exclaimed. The very small cut began to draw blood.

"Christ Almighty, that is sharp!" Mr. Bell grimaced. He yelled into the next room. "Lucy dear, could you bring me a small piece of cloth and some turpentine!?"

John Senior put pressure on the cut and then returned his attention to his son. "Williams, I want you to return these pins to where you found them. It's none of our business. And we mind our own business in this family."

Williams didn't respond at first. John Senior asked more sternly, "You hear?"

"Yes sir," Williams said dejectedly.

"I didn't raise any grave robbers. You have to learn some respect for the dead. You wouldn't want a couple of people messing with your body once you've passed, would you? Do you understand me?"

"Yes, Sir," the boy replied meekly. "Also, I want you to stay out of those caves. No good can come from messing around in them. They're dangerous." "Yes, sir, Father." Williams left the table.

"Here you go, honey," Mrs. Bell said as she handed her husband a small damp cloth. John Bell wiped the blood from his hand before wrapping it in the cloth.

Mrs. Bell patted her husband's hand and said, "Are you okay, honey?"

"I'm fine, but it hurts pretty bad, for such a tiny cut." Mrs. Bell smiled at her husband, thinking he was acting like a baby over such a small cut. She said, "Keep it wrapped and it should heal in a couple of days."

The next day, John Junior and Williams were walking home along the dirt road after a jaunt into town when a horse-drawn buggy came barreling up the dirt road, leaving a trail of dust behind. The buggy seemed to be in an awfully big hurry, and the horse was sweating heavily from being driven hard for quite a while. The horse reared up a bit as the black buggy roared toward the boys. Then it came to a halt right in front of them.

Both young men politely said, "Hello, Mrs. Batts."

"Hello, boys," the old lady said. "I heard you all were poking around a cave the other day and digging up things that weren't yours."

Williams responded, "We weren't digging up anything. It was an accident. The stump gave way and I fell into a hole."

"Well," the old Batts said, "You boys shouldn't be sticking your noses where they don't belong. For all you know, you might have dug up something that doesn't want to be disturbed."

The driver of the buggy yelled "giddyap" and her buggy passed the boys, headed directly for the church. Clouds of dust burst up from the wheels of the carriage as old lady Batts commanded her driver to slide the vehicle to a stop in front of the church house.

Inside John Bell sat before the church panel as the preacher led a group discussion. The quiet conversation continued until Kate Batts walked in. The group turned to greet her.

"You're late, Mrs. Batts."

"Well," the sullen woman spat out, "John Bell's sons were walking in the middle of the road and wouldn't get out of my way." John Senior looked up at the old woman and shook his head in disgust. He knew Batts wasn't telling the truth about his sons.

The preacher began, "Mr. Bell, Mrs. Batts has brought the matter of a real estate transaction between yourself and the Batts to our attention. She claims that you have cheated them on the purchase and it is our duty to investigate. We all know that you are a decent, church-going man. You are well-respected around this community, and this is the first time any sort of grievance has been filed against you. We simply want to get to the bottom of this."

John Bell stood and cleared his throat. Taking a deep breath, he stood tall and proud. "Like I have said before, gentlemen, I purchased, fair and square, the land from Kate Batts's husband. We agreed on the size of the land and the price. Thereafter, as agreed, I handed over one hundred and twenty dollars. End of story. There was no trickery or manipulation—it was a straightforward transaction between two men."

John Senior nodded his head in a manner that suggested that was all he had to say. The preacher arose. "Thank you for your statement. John, you do understand that we will be speaking with several others who perhaps witnessed the deal take place?"

Kate Batts stamped her foot and shouted out. "That's it! I demand an investigation. You cheated me, John Bell," the cranky old woman pointed a gnarled finger at John as her voice escalated in agitation and hatred. "You can't get away with this, you shyster John Bell. You think you are smarter than everybody else!"

Mrs. Batts stamped her other foot in anger and continued. "Well, I'll show you what smart really is! You're not going to get away with this!"

Kate Batts was so upset by that time that she stamped both feet at once, which appeared to make her bounce up and down. Then the old curmudgeon stormed out of the church, so mad she seemed to slobber at the mouth like a rabid dog.

The preacher smiled at the group and said, "Thank you all for coming today. Have a safe trip home. God bless you all."

John Bell, ever the Southern gentleman, politely shook hands with the preacher. "Thank you, Reverend, for all that you have done. Thanks again for your concern and your time."

The other men serving on the panel watched John Bell leave and then mulled around together, whispering and discussing the goings-on.

CHAPTER 8

THE NEXT DAY the sun shone brilliantly in the crystal blue Middle Tennessee sky. Crickets and other critters of the same ilk sent a cascade of musical noises throughout the gentle countryside.

Regardless of the dispute with Mrs. Batts that the church leaders were investigating, life went on at the farm. John Bell headed out to the fields with mules in tow and began to plow that day. It was hard work, and he labored all day long. Having packed a sack lunch of fried chicken and whole potatoes, John took time to say a prayer of thanks to the Lord before he ate at noon. Then he started up his plowing again that afternoon. Life was hard, and the work was never done. Sunset arrived as a beautiful display of reds, purples and oranges across the Southern sky. The unusual nature and lovely hues of the sky made John Bell pause. He wiped his brow with his handkerchief and gazed off into the distance.

Far away, an enormous bird caught his attention. Placing his 'kerchief back in his pocket, John held his hand to his brow to watched the bird's flight.

It circled a bit in the distance and then started to fly directly toward John. The bizarre nature of the creature compelled John to continue staring as it landed on a nearby fence row.

As John looked at the strange visitor, he was suddenly aware that the bird had facial features almost like a human. The huge avian anomaly sat on the fence and stared directly at John Bell. Although John was nervous, almost in a panic, he stared without blinking at the beast. Despite the horror that John Bell felt creeping over his soul, he calmly walked back to his house and got his rifle. He opened a box of shells that he and Williams had hand-loaded the previous winter. John fumbled the cartridges a bit because of his trembling hands. Still he managed to load the rifle.

Without talking to anyone, he shouldered the weapon and quickly strode back to the field, where the bird still sat astride the fence, staring at him. John took aim, held his breath, and fired a shot at the feathery varmint. Flocks of crows, blue jays and sparrows flew up into the air from the loudness of the report, but not that odd bird. It never flinched.

Nervous and unsure of what to do, John walked closer to obtain a better shot. When he had the bizarre bird directly in his cross-hairs, John hesitated a bit, deeply unsettled, as he studied the face of the creature. The bird seemed to mock John Bell as it left its perch and slowly flew away. John didn't fire as it faded away into the afternoon haze.

John Bell trembled mightily as he pulled the rifle off his shoulder and rested it on the ground. It was slowly turning from dusk into evening, and the seriously shaken John Bell looked around. Thankfully, he concluded, there was no one else that witnessed the bizarre event.

John Bell Senior said little at dinner and refused to respond to his wife's worried questions—she sensed that something had happened. John refused to tell his family about the horrific bird and finally headed off to bed and fell into a fitful sleep. John awoke early the next day, and, as with all farm families, was faced with more of the same. A beautiful dawn brought realization that a farmer's work is never done, and John Senior once more readied himself. John Senior and Junior ate breakfast and soon found themselves working together, fixing fences, hoeing, and readying the barn for hay. Junior was still excited about his exploits with the greatest general of that time. So he described some of his exploits to his dad, trying not to brag, yet doing so just the same. John Senior was still trying to reconcile the meaning of the horrifying fowl he tried to shoot the previous afternoon. He really wasn't in the mood to hear all of that. Not wanting to be rude, he grunted out an occasional "okay" and "really" and caught only every tenth word of what his son was saying.

"Then General Jackson had us retreat," John Junior explained, walking back a few steps with his hoe serving as a rifle. "But just for a moment. It turns out it was a decoy maneuver. Let me tell you, the Redcoats played sucker and walked right into it. Ol' Hickory is a whale of a general—he's a genius."

Junior smiled about the thought of the mighty general and his army's exploits fighting the British and the Indians. Noticing his father's silence, Junior tried to discern what might be worrying him.

Unable to find any simple explanation for his father's mood, Junior cautiously asked, "Is something the matter, Father?"

John Senior stopped working and turned to his son. A worried, harrowing look of concern contorted every inch of his weathered but handsome face.

He leaned on his hoe for support for a second, then responded. "Son, I'm fine. I'd just like to finish up a little early today, that's all," he said as he leaned harder on his hoe for support.

Then John stopped and thought better of not saying anything to his son. Slowly, the father confided in his son. "Junior, have you noticed anything unusual around here, in town, or the house?"

John Junior, still with hoe in hand, shook his head and said, "Nothing that I can think of, sir. Why do you ask?" "No reason, really, I just saw this very, very strange-looking bird yesterday,"

Junior interrupted his father. "Speaking of strange things . . ." he pointed with an outstretched hand past his father's shoulder. John turned to see a very large and sinister rabbit. The ferocious-looking hare was at least three times the size of a normal rabbit. It was endowed with an abnormally long snout and sharp, gnarled teeth. "Father, what is that thing?"

"I don't know son." The monster rabbit began to move closer to them.

John Bell whispered to his son. "Junior?" John Bell whispered so as not to rile the creature.

"Yes, sir?" Junior replied as quietly as possible.

"Get the shotgun from the house. It is behind the. . . " Junior was gone before he finished his sentence.

With a long, striding walk, Junior began to put distance between himself and the fanged rabbit before breaking into a full-scale run. Grabbing the weapon, he dashed back toward his father. When John Junior returned to the field with the shotgun, he handed it to his dad and tried to catch his breath, bending at the waist and breathing heavily.

"Is it loaded?" John Senior asked of his exhausted son.

"Yes, sir," John Junior gasped out. "Two shots."

John Senior took aim, setting the rabbit in his sight. He fired squarely at it, but missed. The rabbit stopped in its tracks and actually looked at him, then unbelievably it smiled through those crooked, yellow, fangs.

"Unbelievable," John Senior said to himself as he took aim

and pulled the trigger a second time. He missed again! That time the humongous rabbit took off and disappeared in the woods.

"What was that?" Junior asked of his dad, finally able to talk plainly.

"Son, I don't know. But I do know that I never want to see it ever again." John Senior looked at his son in dead earnestness. "This is between me and you, John Junior. Do you swear? I don't want your mother to be upset."

"Yes sir, I promise." Junior said. Then, looking back at his father with utmost respect in his voice, "Sir, I don't believe anyone would believe me if I were to tell them about what happened today anyway!"

That same day, Betsy Bell had some chores to do. Her work carried her to a lane that ran through the Bell forest. Walking alone in the dark woods near the farm, she stopped to rest beside the small stream. Before she continued her journey, she paused to watch the gentle water run.

Betsy looked down the river a ways and saw something white hanging in a tree, a light-colored piece of cloth dangling from a rope. It was a far way off, and she squinted to get a better view. In the dim light of the woods, she still couldn't quite make out what the object was. To obtain a better view, young Betsy Bell rose from her comfortable seat on the old log next to the stream and slowly walked toward the white object. As she got closer, her hand instinctively covered her mouth. Young Betsy tried to suppress a scream.

It was a dead woman. The body had a rope around its neck and was hanging from a thick tree limb! Betsy tried to scream, but nothing came out. Tears of horror flowed from her eyes. Betsy felt paralyzed with fear, but she slowly started to walk anyway, her hand still covering her mouth in terror.

The dead woman's eyes flashed open. The decaying corpse

looked directly into Betsy's eyes. In the most horrible voice Betsy had ever heard it said, "Betsy Bell, I have come to kill your father."

That time Betsy did scream. So loud were her screams that the birds exploded from the nearby brambles. Dozens of different birds flew toward the bright sun above to escape the dark forest. Betsy decided that was a good idea and turned and ran as fast as her young legs could carry her. She tripped and fell a couple of times, scraping her hands and knees. Each time, the terror that gripped her forced her to get up, and Betsy ran that much harder.

Junior and John Senior heard her screams and started running for the woods.

Betsy continued to scream as she ran. The thick woods played havoc with the men trying to find the horrified girl. They finally spotted Betsy in the distance, and ran to her side.

Betsy was gasping for breath. As she tried to wipe away the tears streaming down her face, they mixed with the dirt on her hands and covered her face with streaks of mud.

"What is it, girl?" her father demanded as he wiped the mud off his daughter's face. Betsy collapsed into her father's arms.

"Father, Father, there is a. . ." Betsy gasped and choked on her words from hysteria and near exhaustion. John Senior continued to support his daughter, but prodded her to talk. "Betsy, what happened?"

Still gasping with every breath, Betsy was finally able to croak out, "There is a dead woman hanging from a tree by the stream." Then Betsy choked back more tears as she said, "The lady is hanging by a rope around her neck." Betsy shook with horror at the thought of the corpse she saw dangling in front of her. She continued, her face buried in her hands. "Father, she is hanging from that old oak tree that has been hit by lightning." Then Betsy wailed in despair. "Father, the dead woman told me. . ." Betsy continued to hold her tear-soaked face in her hands and then hesitated, as if she couldn't speak the horrible truth.

"Go ahead, Betsy, tell me!" John Senior implored, holding his daughter tightly.

Betsy looked up into her father's eyes and moaned out, "Father, she said she is going . . . to kill you!"

John and Junior looked at each other in dismay. "Do you know how to find her?" John Senior asked, still clutching his daughter tightly.

Betsy nodded her head and snuffled, "Yes." The revulsion at what she saw kept Betsy from doing anything but shaking and holding her head in her hands.

"Will you take us to her, Betsy?" John Senior adamantly asked. When Betsy said nothing, he gently shook her to gain her attention. "Betsy, take us to her!"

John and his son held tightly to the still-distressed girl and began to gently guide her in the direction from which she had run.

Betsy regained some semblance of composure and then led the way, pulling at her father's and brother's strong arms that were now holding her back. John Junior, Betsy and their father clawed their way through the brambles, shrubs and low-lying branches of the Bell woods, clambering in the direction where Betsy saw the horrific sight.

When Betsy began to recognize some of the surroundings where she saw the dead woman hanging from the tree, she started to hurry. Finally Betsy reached the old log in the woods where she rested. Betsy pointed to the spot in the woods ahead where the hideous, decaying dead woman was hanging.

Betsy looked confused. She looked one way then another. Her tear-stained eyes stabbed in every direction. She was searching frantically, madly for the dead woman who had spoken to her.

"What is it, Betsy?" John Senior asked. "Where is she?"

Betsy ripped herself from their grasp and gasped, "She was there. She was right there." She scurried off, looking along the stream where she had rested. The two men looked around for awhile with her. Finally, they realized their search was futile. A dead, decaying woman hanging from a tree and talking should not be very hard to find. The smell alone should have led them to the general location.

John Senior looked at his daughter compassionately. "There is nothing here, Betsy," he said.

Betsy was bewildered, "She was here, Father. She was right here." Betsy was hysterical because she knew if she didn't find the dead lady, they would think she had lost her mind. "There!" Betsy screamed as she pointed to an oak at least a century old. Betsy's tears burst out again as she looked up into the very tree where the dead woman had spoken to her. "This is it, Father!!" Betsy screamed in desperation. She dashed to the trunk of the old oak. She triumphantly pointed to an old lightning scar that had ripped open the trunk of the mighty oak.

"See, Father, I know this is it. Look where lightning has hurt the trunk of the tree," Betsy proclaimed as she took her right hand and gently caressed the old gnash twisting along the length of the oak's trunk. The wound was made years ago, the bark split open by a hundred million volts of power from the lightning bolt that embraced the oak. As Betsy touched the wounded trunk, she pleaded her case, pulling her father and brother by the hand to the base of the oak tree.

"This is the place, I swear!" Betsy said, her voice trembling, tears welling up again in her eyes. The whimpering girl ran her hand over the trunk again and again, as if the touch of the rough bark could prove that she was not going insane.

"Look, Father, look, Brother," Betsy shouted. "She was hanging from that very limb!" Betsy proclaimed as she pointed to a very large branch, as thick around as a man's waist.

"I believe you, Daughter," John said as he held her tight.

"I believe you, Sister," Junior said as he joined his dad in holding onto Betsy. The two men looked at each other with deep fear, not knowing what was going on. But they believed her. Hadn't they too witnessed something that defied explanation?

Together the threesome walk home arm in arm, silent and fearful. Individually, collectively, and in silence, John Senior, John Junior and Betsy Bell all wondered as they walked home, "What in the name of all that is holy and good is going on?"

Nashville boys get the works from the Bell Witch as they try to get away.

Photograph courtesy of Big River Pictures

Young men from Nashville try to find the Bell Witch in 1935.

Photograph courtesy of Big River Pictures

Townspeople enjoy great music at John Bell's yearly hoedown.

Photograph courtesy of Big River Pictures

Williams Bell shows off his treasure in the schoolhouse.

John Bell's family and townspeople gather at his grave for the funeral.

John Bell Jr.'s horse blocks the road as Kate Batts and driver try to pass.

Photograph courtesy of Big River Pictures

John Bell and Kate Batts try to come to an agreement at the church.

Photograph courtesy of Big River Pictures

Love-struck Joshua Gardner tries for Betsy Bell's hand in marriage.

Photograph courtesy of Big River Pictures

Professor Powell tries to court Betsy Bell after school is out.

Betsy Bell tells Joshua Gardner they can never get married.

Photograph courtesy of Big River Pictures

Joshua Gardner heads home on horseback.

Photograph courtesy of Big River Pictures

Betsy Bell finally gets a moment of peace from the Bell Witch.

John and Lucy Bell enjoy the summer day.

Photograph courtesy of Big River Pictures

"Kate," the Bell Witch, enters John Bell's bedroom with a bottle of poison.

Photograph courtesy of Big River Pictures

The Bell family and the church members hear the witch talk and sing during a church service.

Photograph courtesy of Big River Pictures

Joshua Gardner and Betsy Bell sneak away for a romantic picnic in the forest.

Photograph courtesy of Big River Pictures

Betsy Bell and Joshua Gardner fall in love on the Bell farm.

Photograph courtesy of Big River Pictures

Kate Batts tries to collect the rest of her money from John Bell.

Photograph courtesy of Big River Pictures

John Bell tells his son, Williams, that he will be the man of the house soon.

Photograph courtesy of Big River Pictures

Lucy comforts John after a confrontation with the Bell Witch.

Photograph courtesy of Big River Pictures

Sons Williams and John Jr. comfort their mother, Lucy Bell.

Photograph courtesy of Big River Pictures

John Bell speaks to his family at the dinner table.

Photograph courtesy of Big River Pictures

Williams Bell makes a discovery in a cave under the Bell farm.

Photograph courtesy of Big River Pictures

Professor Powell comforts Betsy Bell.

Photograph courtesy of Big River Pictures

John Bell Jr. and John Bell search for the cause of strange noises heard around the Bell house.

Photograph courtesy of Big River Pictures

Joshua Gardener meets up with Betsy Bell for some summer courting.

Photograph courtesy of Big River Pictures

Joshua Gardner and Williams Bell discuss the day's chores on the Bell house porch.

Photograph courtesy of Big River Pictures

While walking in the woods, Betsy Bell comes face to face with a girl hanging in a tree.

Photograph courtesy of Big River Pictures

Lucy Bell comforts John Bell after a night of terror.

Photograph courtesy of Big River Pictures

Joshua Gardener proposes to Betsy in the barn.

Betsy Bell and Joshua Gardner hold hands.

Photograph courtesy of Big River Pictures

Williams Bell is in trouble with Professor Powell.

John Bell's daughter, Betsy, realizes she can never get away from the Bell Witch.

Photograph courtesy of Big River Pictures

Betsy Bell sneaks a tender kiss from Joshua behind the Bell barn.

Lucy Bell and daughter, Betsy, discuss future plans.

CHAPTER **9**

THE NEXT NIGHT a somber silence overtook the Bell house. Each family member coped with the situation in a different way. John Bell smoked a cigar as he carved a wooden cross. Every now and then he blew a smoke ring. His need for a cross was self-evident. And he had learned from Cherokee legend that tobacco has special power over evil. Ordinarily not a smoker, tonight John Bell smoked with a passion.

John Junior cleaned out the shotgun. He used wadding from a cotton bale that General Jackson personally bought for his battalion in New Orleans.

Betsy and Lucy sewed, working on stockings, socks and light colored scarves. Williams slept on the floor. Unbeknownst to himself, Williams was snoring loudly, which brought comfort to the rest of the Bell family, otherwise distraught by the events of the past few days.

A small pebble pecked against the windowpane. Betsy was the only one to notice it, because it was intended to get her attention.

"May I be excused, Father?" Betsy asked politely.

John Bell looked up from his carving and saw his daughter's face through a ringlet of smoke.

"Yes, you may, Betsy."

Unasked, Betsy demurely stated, "I am going to my room for a while." John Senior smiled a knowing smile; perhaps he, too, actually noticed the small pebble that glanced off the windowpane. "Okay, Betsy, but don't go wandering far from the house," he said.

Betsy smiled sweetly as she said, "Yes, Father."

After being excused, Betsy ran up the stairs, into her room and out onto the upstairs balcony. She gently shut the door behind her and looked over the rail of the balcony. Joshua emerged from the side of the house by a gold-tipped juniper.

In a whisper, Joshua Gardner inquired, "Betsy, my love?"

"Is that you, Joshua?" Betsy whispered into the night.

"It's me," Joshua replied sweetly.

Betsy whispered so low as to be barely audible. "I can't go out tonight, Joshua. My father told me to stay close to the house."

"Betsy, that's all right. I should be getting home as well. My horse is tied up down the way. I did not want your father to hear me coming up, but I had to see you tonight. Are you okay, Betsy?" Joshua stopped speaking for just a second to measure his words. "To be honest, you've been acting strange lately."

Betsy whispered back, "Something strange has been going on, Joshua, but I can't talk about it now."

"Okay," Joshua said in an understanding voice. "Some other time then."

Betsy whispered back into the night, "Will you be back at the schoolhouse tomorrow, Joshua?"

"Betsy, I've been thinking about not going back anymore," Joshua responded.

"Joshua, I don't understand, why would you do something like that?" Betsy asked, trying not to let her voice show that she was upset.

"I don't think Professor Powell likes me very much, Betsy," Joshua whispered again.

"Of course he likes you, Joshua," Betsy exclaimed in as loud a voice as she dared.

"I just got a gut feeling he don't," Joshua replied, trying not to show the discontent he felt with the direction the conversation was going.

"Joshua, please come tomorrow. I need to see you. I have to see you."

"Okay, Betsy, then I'll be there for you," Joshua responded, his spirits rising because it was obvious Betsy wanted to see him.

"Thank you, Joshua," Betsy said. "Thank you so much."

"Tomorrow then, Betsy," Joshua whispered into the night.

Betsy replied, "Tomorrow, Joshua."

He blew Betsy a kiss and then headed off into the darkness. Betsy watched him walk away, smiling to herself. She was turning to go back into her bedroom when she stopped in her tracks. Something caught her attention. Betsy squinted her eyes and stared across the darkening landscape of the Bell family farm. Suddenly she realized it was a woman. A woman draped in white, wearing nothing but white, wispy clothing that glided behind her in the evening. The woman was almost waltzing, almost floating across the land. She appeared to be an older woman; Betsy couldn't be sure because she was so far away.

John Bell stepped out onto the porch, looking for his daughter.

"Betsy dear?" John Senior spoke in a hushed tone.

"Father! There is a woman walking across the farm!" she said urgently.

John Senior stared out across his farm. He, too, saw a

woman—or an apparition of a woman, her flowing white clothes so wispy as to be almost transparent. John Senior put his arm around his daughter, subconsciously trying to keep her safe. They were stunned as they stood together watching the woman disappear into the evening. It was so strange: Even though she was not walking away from them, she was slowly disappearing from their sight.

As the apparition slowly vanished, Junior and Lucy Bell climbed to the balcony and joined Betsy and John Senior in shocked silence.

Lucy Bell looked up at her husband with an extremely worried look on her face. "What is it, John?"

John Senior made eye contact with his son, John Junior. Father and son knew they had just witnessed another bizarre sighting. Both had very perplexed expressions on their faces.

John Senior looked down at his wife; the seriousness of his face made her draw back a bit. "Lucy, let's get everybody downstairs. We need to talk." Lucy nodded in agreement. "Children, let's gather downstairs," she said. They went quietly into the sitting room. The lanterns were turned up very bright in the small room, which served as a parlor. The Bell family sat in a semicircle listening to their father speak. John paced back and forth. The bewildered man didn't really know where to start, but he decided just to plow forward.

"Children . . . Lucy," John Senior stopped pacing long enough to smile at his wife. "There have been some bizarre things happening around here the last couple of days."

John Senior continued to pace back and forth in front of his family. Lucy, Junior, Betsy and Williams sat with stone faces, staring at their father as he continued relentlessly pacing back and forth.

John stopped and looked them all directly in the eyes. Then, commandingly, he said, "I do not want any of you to leave this house alone." John Senior's tone became increasingly stern. "Pair up when you walk to school, or if you are working on the farm. Never be alone."

Williams glanced around at his family with a troubled look on his face. "Father, is there something wrong?"

John Senior stopped his pacing and paused to reflect. "I'm not sure yet, Williams. I just want you all to be safe and be aware. So don't . . ." John was cut off from his explanation in mid-sentence by a loud growling sound coming from the outside. The entire family looked toward the south end of the house, the area from which the noise was coming. Instantly, a scratching reverberation came from the opposite end of the house.

John whirled around toward the direction of the noise and shouted, "Junior, grab the shotguns!"

"Don't go out there, John," Lucy pleaded with her husband. "John, it's just an animal. It will go away," she said, her voice quivering with fear for her husband.

Junior grabbed two shotguns and gave one to his father. The two men stormed out the front door ready to fire. Outside, they decided to split up. John tiptoed to one corner of the house. He quickly looked around the corner with his gun cocked and ready to fire. There was no animal, nothing. Junior ran to the other end of the house. He rounded the corner and aimed, ready to fire at any intruder. Again, there was nothing.

The Bell men tiptoed around to the back of the house. They were sure the animal was back there. They stopped behind the corner and simultaneously spun around ready to shoot. There was no animal. They stood there a moment with their weapons pointed at one another, then headed back into the house.

The family was waiting for the men. Williams looked up at his older brother and father. "What was it?"

John said, "It must have run away." Junior added, "We didn't see anything, nothing at all."

Quietly clutching her Bible, Lucy said, "I told you two not to go. . . .

The loud sound of flapping wings echoed through the house, like the wings of a giant bird. Betsy screamed with fright as the flapping grew louder. The noise went around the house. They all ducked as the unseen bird flew overhead.

Mother Lucy hugged Williams and Betsy to her body. John followed the flapping noise around the house, although there was no sign of the noise's source. Hysteria gripped the group, then as quickly as the commotion started, it stopped. No one said a word or flinched. Though the family was in shock and dismayed, they soon agreed to go about their business and get ready for bed.

Later that night, Williams and Junior were saying their prayers. They had never prayed so hard in their whole lives, or maybe, in Williams's life. Junior prayed very hard, just as hard when he fought alongside General Jackson in New Orleans. Junior had faced death and he knew how to pray . . . and mean it.

In the next room, Lucy and John also prayed. They took a moment to blow out the candles together before they grasped each other's hands and went to bed. Betsy reluctantly went back to her bedroom. She peeled the quilts off her bed and, with hesitation, blew out the candle on her nightstand next to the window.

Later that evening, a penetrating quiet lowered over the Bell house. The moonlight filtered in through the windows. Considering the distressful nature of the commotion earlier that night, everyone was sleeping soundly. Betsy was unaware when a mysterious, milky green light and silky jade smoke began to appear in her closet and then filter under the door.

Somehow, perhaps subconsciously, Betsy rolled to the side of the bed where the emerald apparition approached her. Betsy tossed and mumbled in her sleep; the green light receded into the closet. Betsy rolled over and away from the closet, and the ominous emerald illumination glided back over the floor and covered Betsy.

The ghost whispered into Betsy's ear, "Betsy, Betsy, my dear." The emerald green fog dissolved and disappeared under the closet door.

Betsy awoke with a start, although she felt as if she was in a dream. Her heart racing, she glanced around the room rapidly. She was certain she heard someone speaking to her. Betsy calmed down and assumed the voice she heard was a dream or an imagination. Betsy returned to sleep.

Dawn in Adams, Tennessee, could be spectacular. It was that morning. With all the goings-on in the Bell family, no one noticed the beautiful blazing orange hues that radiated from the epicenter of the brilliant early-morning sun. Betsy certainly didn't as she sat on the porch the next morning. Neither did brother Williams as he walked up to Betsy after some morning chores.

"Betsy, are you okay?" Williams asked in a concerned, brotherly voice.

Betsy's eyes welled up slightly with tears, but they did not run down her cheeks as she maintained her composure. "I'm okay, brother, but I am so worried about Father!" Betsy declared in a slow, but resolute voice, pausing to rub her eyes with her shirtsleeve. "I saw what I saw yesterday, Williams."

"I believe you! And last night!" Williams spoke in a controlled whisper, hoping not to be heard by his mother or father.

"Go on, Williams," Betsy shushed her little brother away. "We'll be fine, Father will be fine; let's go about our chores and lives like we're supposed to. Let's try not to upset Mother and Father."

Williams nodded his head and whispered, "You're right, Sis." He headed out to the fields to start working as usual.

Later that night, Williams was exhausted from a full day of hard labor. He was hot and sweaty, so he took a relaxing, warm bath. The gentle vapors of the bath and the lye soap washed the feelings of uncertainty away from him. He went to bed. Sleep flooded over him because of his extreme exhaustion. After midnight, his sheets were slowly pulled down from his body, not waking him. He was cool without the covers on him and he woke up. Williams grabbed the sheets and pulled them back up to where he liked them, neck level. He prepared to return to sleep, as he groggily grasped his sheets in his closed fists.

Whack. The sheets and flimsy coverlet quilt were ripped from his hands so violently that the noise reverberated throughout the room. Williams simply kept his eyes closed as tight as he could and prayed as hard as he ever had before in his young life. Williams's young body trembled in fear, and one lone teardrop trickled down his cheek, dangled there and then dropped to the sheet, where it turned to blood. The crimson droplet was slowly absorbed into the sheet and disappeared as if it had never been present.

The next day again brought the regular chores to the family. Williams struggled to get out of bed, but dutifully did so. The youngster went untold to chop wood and kindling for the breakfast stove. John Bell looked out at his young son, and couldn't help but feel a great pang of sorrow for what his son and family were going through. He didn't know why any of this was happening, and he didn't know what else to do but to go about his business. He did know he wanted to relieve some of his son's anxiety. John Senior strode out to the porch and down to the small woodpile they kept by the house for cookstove kindling.

"Williams."

"What, Father?" Williams smiled a bit at his father as he picked up a stick of wood to split.

"Why don't you go inside and get some sleep this morning?"

"I can't, I have chores to do," the exhausted boy told his caring dad.

"I know you do, son, but you are exhausted, I can tell."

"I didn't sleep very good last night," Williams admitted. "Then go inside and get some sleep, son, I'll take care of this and you can do your chores again tomorrow." Williams dropped the axe to the ground and gratefully returned to the house, where he knew he could get some much-needed sleep. Never before—that is, before this week—did Williams think he would be able to sleep in broad daylight. He did that day.

CHAPTER 10

T HAT DAY PASSED slowly, but thankfully without any upset. After a quiet dinner, John Senior and Lucy retired to bed, hoping for an uneventful evening. It was not to be so. The pinprick wound on John's hand started to bleed. It didn't wake him, but the next morning Lucy and he were shocked by the amount of blood that had soaked the bedsheets. They changed the sheets and cleaned the dressing on the wound in a gritty and determined silence. Their unspoken words said that they loved each other and that they were going to get through this terrible ordeal no matter what it took.

John Bell called his small family to a meeting in the parlor.

"None of your friends know about the problems this family is having, do they?"

Collectively, the group said, "No. No, sir. No."

John Senior paced back and forth over the braided rug that covered the wooden floor. "Family," John Senior started talking, with a worried look on his face. "I hope all of this is over with. I don't know why it started exactly, but I suggest we don't keep it that way. I am going to get to the bottom of this very soon. We don't want our neighbors to think we're involved in witchcraft. And we don't want the church to find out about this. I'll figure this out. In the meantime, let's keep this in the family, strictly to ourselves, okay? Is everyone in agreement?"

Everyone in the group looked at each other and nodded their heads in agreement. Later that very evening, John and Lucy retired to their bedroom. They were both asleep when the shutter outside their window slowly banged against the house. John thought he was dreaming, but he heard a voice calling from downstairs. "John . . ." came the whispered voice. "John . . ."

John realized that he was awake and that he was hearing something; what he heard, he didn't know. The shutter banged slowly, repeatedly, against the wall. Still, he knew he heard a voice.

He got to his feet, trying to keep quiet so he didn't awaken his wife or his children. He got one of the lit candles from the wall, and approached the staircase.

"John . . ." the voice called out in a low whisper again. Now John Bell was awake enough to be sure that he heard it.

"Oh John . . ." the voice whispered, but in a wailing manner.

He started down the staircase. He took each step slowly, peering over the railing to see if there was someone or something downstairs. It had begun to rain outside, and the moisture blew through the barely open window, almost blowing out his candle. He shut the window quietly and looked at his scared reflection in the mirror on the wall.

At that instant, a large bolt of lightning revealed a woman's reflection in the mirror. She was standing directly behind him! Panic-stricken, he whirled around, but there was no one there. Another lightning bolt flashed across the sky, illuminating the entire room. There was nothing, certainly no sign of any person in the room. John took a deep breath and slowly headed back upstairs.

Swoosh. A flying sound buzzed over his head and he felt something wispy slide by his face. He ducked instinctively, held the candle above his head and surveyed the staircase. There was still nothing there. Shaken by the experience, John walked slowly back up the staircase, holding onto the railing for dear life.

The next morning, Lucy awakened and was actually frightened that her husband was not in bed beside her. She scurried downstairs and was relieved to find him sitting in the kitchen. He was hard at work, whittling a wooden cross.

Lucy looked down at her husband's frantic work and asked reluctantly, "John, did something happen last night while I was sleeping?"

"Something or someone got violent last night. It almost knocked me down," John responded, his hands continuing their busy work, but trembling just the same.

"But Lucy, there was nothing there!"

Lucy walked to her husband and knelt by his side, not wanting to interrupt what he was doing, even though she wished he would stop his frantic whittling. "John, darling, maybe we need to tell someone."

John stopped his work, and with a pained look on his face, asked of his wife, "And then what, Lucy?" John shook his head in dismay and looked down at the wooden cross in his hands.

"Do you have any idea how people will look at us? I'd lose all of my customers, and we'd lose all of our friends." Such was the fear of witchcraft and witches and demons in their small town.

"Our children would be taunted at school. And darling, we wouldn't be allowed in our own church. People are already looking at me strangely. This Batts family thing has been a harrowing ordeal."

Lucy nodded as she got up and put her arms around her

husband. Then she asked, "What are we going to do then, John?"

"Lucy, just give me a little while longer . . . I'll try to figure it out."

CHAPTER 11

PROFESSOR POWELL GREETED the last class of the year with the same irascible nature that he greeted the first class. He took the chalk and scratched it across the blackboard to garner everyone's attention.

Soon everyone was following Professor Powell's directions and working hard on their arithmetic.

Williams Bell's efforts to stay awake were failing. He blinked his eyes constantly, his head jerking backward as he almost nodded off every few minutes.

In the very last row of the class, Betsy Bell had also nodded off. Undaunted by the Professor, she crossed her arms over her desk and fell into a deep slumber. Betsy knew she was Professor Powell's favorite student, so she didn't fear his wrath.

Joshua sat right next to her, as he did every day. It made him feel very secure to watch over his betrothed-to-be every day at school. A puzzled look came over Joshua's face as he stared at the beautiful young Betsy. She roused a bit from her sleep and turned her head over toward Joshua. He saw some light red marks outlined on his beautiful young girlfriend's face. It looked as if someone had slapped her extremely hard. Already Joshua was worried about Betsy; now he felt his skin crawl with concern. The imprint of a hand across Betsy's face was bold enough that it was unmistakable.

Professor Powell had always been lenient with his favorite pupil, but now her deep slumber, watched over by Joshua, upset the grumpy and indignant Professor.

POW. Professor Powell slammed his math book against the podium so loudly it awakened Betsy. "I am going to allow all of you to leave a bit early today, all but Betsy Bell."

He continued: "Betsy Bell, could I see you at my desk?" the Professor asked boldly. "Everyone else is dismissed. I will see all of you later."

Betsy shyly walked forward to where the Professor sat.

"Betsy, I am displeased with you. There is no sleeping during school hours," the Professor scolded. "I'm sorry, Professor. I did not get much sleep last night, that's all."

"Well, Betsy, what were you doing that prevented you from getting to sleep?"

"Nothing, sir," Betsy responded demurely. If the truth be told, she was still sleepy.

"Nothing. I find that hard to believe, Betsy. If you were any other student I would be outraged. I'd be forced to take disciplinary action. But for you, I'm willing to ignore it this one time. You are my best and most important student; I can't have you falling asleep in my class."

"I understand, Professor," Betsy replied, trying not to yawn right in Professor Powell's face.

"Betsy, I am leaving to go up North in a few days and I would like to follow your progress. If you will allow me, I would like permission to write to you. I would like to keep in touch." Professor Powell bit his lower lip as he looked into Betsy's eyes, awaiting her answer.

Betsy replied, "That would be nice, Professor. I always love getting letters."

"Love letters?" the Professor replied, hearing what he wanted from Betsy's reply. "Well, I'll see what I can do."

"Professor," Betsy began to protest gently, thinking he had misunderstood her.

Realizing that he was making his prize student uncomfortable, the Professor retreated a bit from his assertions. "Oh Betsy, I'm just kidding. Well, let's try to not sleep through the summer."

"It won't happen again, Professor," Betsy promised profusely.

Joshua was waiting for Betsy as she left the schoolhouse. Her head was hanging low. "Betsy, don't let the Professor upset you so," Joshua advised.

"Joshua, it's just that he thinks so highly of me."

"Huh," Joshua snorted, "that Professor is not a nice man. I see the way he stares at you."

Betsy shook her head in disagreement, then fell silent. Her mind was far off, worrying about other things. Joshua realized she wasn't paying much attention to him, and it bothered him.

"Betsy, what is the matter with you? Recently you just ain't been yourself," Joshua complained as he dug at the dirt with his shoe.

"Nothing," Betsy said, shaking her head and then repeating softly, "Nothing."

"Why have you been so quiet?"

"Why is everyone always asking me questions? I don't know all the answers to your silly questions," Betsy rebuked him. She started to run off ahead of Joshua. He caught up to her and grabbed her arm. "Betsy, I just want to know what's the matter."

"Nothing's wrong, Joshua." Betsy jerked her arm away. "Leave me alone."

"I am worried about you, Betsy."

"I said, leave me alone, Joshua," Betsy repeated and ran off ahead of him again. Joshua stood there and simply shook his head, confusion taking over as he simply didn't understand what was wrong.

Later that night, the Bells gathered around the dinner table. No one said a word. Everyone ate as rapidly as they could and avoided bad subjects. It was as if they were waiting for the other shoe to drop as they ate in unbearable silence.

John took a bite of cornbread, and suddenly he couldn't swallow. He tried but he couldn't. He took a big gulp of water, but it didn't help. If anything, it hurt as the water simply poured out of his mouth.

"John, are you okay?" Lucy asked. "John, what is wrong?" Lucy pleaded as she got up and ran to her husband's side.

All John could do was hold his throat and choke, his face turning ever redder. He stood up from the table, coughing and choking, still with his hands on his neck. They heard him mutter something.

Lucy asked, "What, John? Tell me what is wrong."

"I can't swallow," John was barely able to get out. He grabbed the glass of water again and took a huge gulp. Again the water rolled out of his mouth.

"What can I do, John?" Lucy begged her husband to let her know how to help him.

Suddenly the whole house began to rattle. The floor buckled; the walls bent in. It was as if an earthquake had exploded beneath Adams, Tennessee. So violent was the shaking that the family fell to their hands and knees.

"What do you want from us?" Betsy Bell screamed.

Just as quickly as the house had started its violent eruptions, it stopped. John Bell was able to swallow. It was as if nothing had happened, and he raised the glass of water to his lips and swallowed freely.

Betsy started crying and her mother consoled her gently in her arms saying, "Now, now, Betsy, it will be okay." Lucy looked over at John as she continued to soothe Betsy. "John, we can't live like this," she said.

The next day, John Bell went to visit James Johnston at his home. The two men sat on the porch. John whittled another wooden cross. Mrs. Johnston came out on the porch to bring both men a cup of warm tea.

John looked up at the plump Mrs. Johnston and said, "Thank you." Mrs. Johnston excused herself, as she had work to do and went back inside.

James Johnston looked at his old friend, and a slight frown came over his face. "Something serious is on your mind, isn't it, John?"

"Yes, James, there is," John Bell allowed as he lowered his cup of tea. "We're friends, aren't we, James?" John asked rhetorically. "Oh my word, John Bell, of course we are," Mr. Johnston said emphatically.

"You wouldn't judge me then, would you?" John Senior asked quietly.

"What is it, John? What is on your mind?" James Johnston asked compassionately as he leaned closer to his friend.

John Bell sighed a heartfelt sigh, but he didn't know what else to do but tell the plain truth. "James, there is evil living in my house, with my family and me. I don't know what it is, and I don't know what it wants, and I don't know how to get rid of it."

James Johnston got a concerned look on his face and cocked his head. "John, what do you mean by evil?" he asked. "James, I am saying there is something in my house. It makes noises so we can't sleep. At first, we thought it was just rats or some kind of animal. Then the children's bed sheets started to get ripped from their beds while they were asleep. They're getting slapped, poked, and their hair pulled."

"My gosh, John, you say your house is haunted by some form of demon?" James Johnston asked, as sympathetically as he could but still with doubt about the veracity of his friend's tale.

John Bell Senior sighed again and looked directly into James Johnston's eyes. "That's what I'm saying."

James Johnston put down his cup of tea, slowly got out of his seat and walked to the side of the porch. He gazed vacantly over his large farm.

"John . . ." James started talking slowly, but was interrupted by his troubled friend. "You don't believe me?" John asked in a hurt manner.

"John, it is not that I don't believe you—" James Johnston stopped in mid-sentence, obviously trying to choose the right words. James turned and looked directly at his friend. "Look, John, I am a god-fearing Christian, and I . . . well . . ." James Johnston struggled to find the right words. He lowered his eyes, then spoke with a more determined and direct tone of voice.

"No, John Bell," he said. "I don't believe you."

John Bell was somewhat taken aback, although not totally surprised by his friend's rebuff. "Look, James, all you have to do is come stay over at my house one night. Just one night. You and Mrs. Johnston can come and stay. Just one night. I just want you to know that I am not crazy." John Bell Senior dropped his eyes a bit to hold off the shame that he felt, a grown man begging a friend to come observe an unbelievable situation so his friend wouldn't think him crazy. "I simply don't know what else to do, James," John concluded as his voice sank lower.

Sensing the despair in his friend's voice, James Johnston considered the request.

"Okay, then John, very well. The missus and I will spend the night in your home, and together, as Christian friends, we'll figure out what the devil has happened that has got you so . . . " James Johnston struggled for the right words, " . . . upset."

John Bell stood up and shook James's hand with an exuberance he hadn't been able to muster in weeks.

"Thank you so much, James. What about tonight?" John Senior asked.

James saw the unbelievable change in his friend's attitude at his simple gesture. He nodded his head and said, "Okay, John, tonight it is."

So that very night the Johnstons loaded up in their horse and buggy and traveled to the Bell farm by way of the Little River Road.

The Johnston family arrived just in time for dinner. They couldn't help but note the quiet, subdued manner in which the Bells took dinner. The occasional "Pass the peas, please" or "Mother, I'd like an extra roll," followed by a simple "thank you" made up the dinner conversation.

Nothing much was said about the strange occurrences that the Johnstons had been invited to observe, but there was no doubt to Mr. and Mrs. Johnston that a pall hung over the Bell household.

Ever the mother—even though the Bell children were not, well, children—Mrs. Bell still tucked Betsy, Williams and John Junior into bed every night. She began with Betsy. As she left the room, she reminded, "Darling daughter, remember to say your prayers." "I will, Mother," came the dutiful reply as Betsy adjusted her goose down pillow. She hoped that tonight she could obtain some semblance of a full night's sleep, she even wished that the witch would haunt the Johnstons tonight, and not her. She knew this was not the Christian way to act, but she was so tired and overwrought, she just couldn't help it.

While Lucy Bell tended to her children, John Bell showed his guests their room downstairs. Before they turned in for the evening, the Johnstons knelt and prayed at the foot of their bed.

James Johnston led the prayer, just as he did every night at their home. "Dear Heavenly Father, thank you for everything that you have given our family. Thank you for the wonderful meal we had for dinner tonight. Lord protect as we sleep. Let us rest in comfort and in peace tonight. Amen."

"Amen," came the dutiful reply from his wife. The night fell darker and darker, and everything was peaceful. The Johnstons pulled the covers to their necks and drifted off to sleep. They lay undisturbed until the small hours of the morning. Silently and slowly as a snake, the thick blanket slid down to their to waists. The cold brought James partially awake, enough to reach down and pull them up again.

"OWWW!" came a howl of protest from Mrs. Johnston. An unseen hand yanked her hair extremely hard. James watched in horror as he saw his wife being dragged around the bed, by what or whom, he couldn't see.

He demanded of the unseen thing attacking his wife, "In God's name, I ask, what do you want of us?!"

James Johnston was slapped hard on the right cheek for his audacity. Then, for good measure, he was slapped on the other cheek. He roared as he was slammed to the floor where he lay stunned. Mrs. Johnston screamed as her hair was pulled by the unseen attacker.

John and Lucy heard the commotion and came running down the steps. Raising the lantern to illuminate the room, they were stunned to see Mrs. Johnston being dragged by the hair while her husband was knocked down every time he tried to get up.

As soon as the Bells entered the room, the attack was over. Mrs. Johnston's hair went limp and she cradled her torn scalp in both hands. Mr. Johnston was rolling on the floor in tremendous pain.

"What in the good name of God was that?" James Johnston shouted as John helped him up off of the floor. "Do you understand now, James?" John asked.

Mr. Johnston was visibly shaken. "I understand that evil is in this house. We are leaving . . . now."

The family just looked at each other as the Johnstons gathered themselves. They didn't try to stop them from leaving; the Bells themselves would have left long ago, but this was home and there was no place to go.

By the time they readied the horse and buggy, Mr. Johnston had recovered somewhat. From the buggy seat, he looked down at his friend.

"John, this is bigger than us. Please let me organize an investigation committee. Let them see what the missus and I just saw. They'll know what to do. John, do this for your family's sake." John Bell shook his head. "James, I'm not sure I want this spreading around the community. People will think we're witches. I can't have that sort of thing hanging over this family. We would be ruined."

James Johnston steadied the horse, uneasy because of the late-night journey and the humans' agitation. It rolled its eyes as if it sensed something at the Bell house. "John, I know what you're saying, but y'all can't keep going on like this. I understand now what you were telling me. But no one else will unless they experience this in person. John, let me get some help. Do it for your children." John heaved a deep sigh. "All right then, James."

The horse was dancing, trying to get on the road. "I'll talk to you tomorrow, John," Johnston said. He flipped the reins and the horse bolted out of the drive and down the road.

The Bell family gathered in the yard with their arms around each other, building their courage to go back inside their house.

CHAPTER 12

IT TOOK JUST a few days to assemble the group. James Johnston was well-respected, and his obvious fear was quite convincing. The men arrived at the Bell farm late one afternoon. John Senior waited in the yard as they came up the road. James Johnston performed the introductions.

"This is Professor Michaels, a religious scholar from Nashville." John Bell Senior shook the slight man's hand. "Thank you for coming to help, Professor," he said, withdrawing his hand from the teacher's limp grasp.

James said, "John, this is Mr. Roberts, a detective from North Carolina." John shook the burly detective's hand. "Thanks for coming such a long way on such a short notice, Mr. Roberts," he said. He turned to the third man. "This is the Reverend Thorne, also from Nashville." James Johnston announced.

"Thank you, also, Brother Thorne," John Senior said as he shook the very tall man's hand. "Welcome, gentlemen, to my home. I wish you were here under better circumstances. Shall we go inside?"

They reconvened in front of the fireplace. Mr. Michaels was the first to speak up. "I must tell you, Mr. Bell, that we are all a bit skeptical, as you can imagine." Before John Senior could say anything, Mr. Roberts spoke up directly and forcefully. "Mr. Bell, I have heard stories like this before, and every one of them has turned out to be a hoax."

John Bell began to reply, but Mr. Thorne interrupted. The tall reverend from Nashville bent down to speak. Everyone strained to hear his low voice. "Mr. Bell, there is always a reasonable explanation for these . . . occurrences."

Professor Michaels added, "Are you sure, Mr. Bell, that it is not your children pulling a prank?"

John Bell finally spoke, politely but forcefully. "Absolutely not, Professor Michaels." His voice was steadfast as he continued. "My children are the most affected by these circumstances. I assure you this is no prank."

James Johnston spoke up. "As I told you, gentlemen, what I witnessed is not the work of man." A heavy silence descended; the five men avoided each other's eyes. John Bell cleared his throat.

"I do ask that all of you gentlemen keep this in strictest confidence. If the good people of Adams hear about any of this. . . ." He paused to choose his words carefully, then decided to leave his sentence unfinished. The men assured him that they would keep everything they saw confidential.

John Bell remembered his manners. "I appreciate you all coming on such very short notice. I think my wife Lucy has supper almost ready. Let's break bread together."

The subdued group sat down to eat. Conversation was pleasant, but everyone labored to keep it up.

After dinner, the men gravely thanked Lucy Bell for her hospitality and retired to the parlor, where they gathered around the fireplace. Lucy brought them coffee and tea, and John passed around a box of cigars. "I grew this tobacco myself," he explained. The men smoked and engaged in forced small talk.

The whole group seemed on edge as they waited. John Bell and James Johnston exchanged looks; they knew they couldn't make anything happen, but they knew they had to convince these men. As the evening wore on, the conversation wore thin. It was well after midnight, and the investigators were checking their watches.

Professor Michaels was the first to speak. Even though he was committed to stay the night, he suggested it was time to end the evening. "I think it is time for me to go," he said as he stretched his tight muscles.

John Bell was aghast. "Mr. Michaels, you can't leave now." He turned to James Johnston, his only ally.

"Aren't you going to stay through the night?" Johnston asked. "We've seen nothing yet."

Michaels shook his head with a knowing smile. "Thank you for your hospitality, Mr. Bell, but I don't believe there's any more to be seen here."

Detective Roberts stood, too. "Yep, another false alarm," he announced. "Just as I expected." The detective concluded, "I am with Mr. Michaels here. It's time to be going."

John Bell begged the men to stay. He and his family were at the end of their rope, and these men were his only hope for resolution. "Please gentlemen, you cannot go."

But the men were insistent and moved toward the door. Detective Roberts turned and tipped his hat. "Good night, Mr.— " he was saying when the front door slammed shut with a bang! Simultaneously a voice came from somewhere overhead and echoed throughout the house: "Just where do you think you are going?"

The five men gasped, looking in every direction. They were alone in the room. "By God, Mr. Bell, who said that?" the Reverend Thorne shouted. Roberts pulled at the doorknob, but it didn't budge.

The voice came again, cold and evil, striking fear into their hearts. "I said that."

Professor Michaels ran to the window, but try as he might he couldn't get it open. The spirit laughed, a chilling sound. "You can't leave now Mr. Michaels."

The Reverend Thorne spoke bravely: "Who are you?"

The answer came in a low voice, "Call me Kate."

John and James were stunned. They had steeled themselves to face a physical attack, but this unexpected voice had unnerved them.

"Where are you, Kate?" Detective Roberts asked.

"Everywhere," the voice moaned. Indeed, the words seemed to come from no one place, but all around them.

Reverend Thorne, made steadfast by his faith, asked, "Are you a witch?"

"I sure am," Kate declared.

"Prove it," Detective Roberts growled, angered by a presence that wouldn't show itself.

In a calculating voice, Kate said coyly, "Detective Roberts, you recently killed a man and used your position to cover it up."

"That is lunacy!" the detective swore, but his face revealed that the witch had clearly touched a nerve.

"And you, Professor Michaels, you have been stealing books and selling them." The tall Professor was shocked but didn't say a word in rebuttal.

"And you, Preacher Thorne," the voice cooed, "You're talking money from the church's collection basket . . . a lot of money." The thin preacher's face turned completely white, but he said not a word.

Whether these revelations were true was known only to the accused, but clearly, Kate the witch had their undivided attention.

"What . . . what are you going to do with us?" Reverend Thorne stammered.

Kate responded in her most civil voice, "My purpose is not to harm you gentlemen. But I am going to kill Mr. John Bell."

They all turned to stare at John Bell in horror. He felt wetness on his palm and held his hand up before him. The pinprick was bleeding profusely. John Senior tried to wrap the wound tighter but the ragged cloth quickly soaked through with bright red blood.

Just then, the front door swung wide open, as if Kate was bidding them farewell. The five men wasted no time escaping the house. They got their horses saddled in record time.

"I gather you gentlemen believe me now," John Bell declared.

Professor Michaels looked down from his buggy seat. "There must be some explanation," he said, almost pleadingly. "I would like to inform some scholars in Nashville what I've witnessed here. Do I have your permission, Mr. Bell?"

"Do what you must," John Bell declared with resignation. Detective Roberts echoed Mr. Michaels's thoughts. "Mr. Bell, there was a reasonable explanation for all of this. I am unable to identify it at the present time. I am headed home to North Carolina and will return with more resources."

John Bell was no closer to a solution than before they came. "What am I supposed to do until then?" he asked plaintively.

The Reverend Thorne placed his hand on John Senior's shoulder, "Pray Brother Bell. Pray to our Lord. He'll hear your prayers—and answer them."

A noise from the house caused them all to turn and look. They heard the cackling voice of the witch, laughing hysterically from inside the Bell home. That was the last straw for the investigators. They whipped their horses and took off at a gallop.

John Bell stood alone. He squared his shoulders and strode back into his home, surrounded by the witch's laughter. He grabbed the door with his bloody hand and slammed it with all his might.

CHAPTER 13

THE NEXT DAY, John Senior was desperate enough to seek support from the town's leaders. He visited privately with his own preacher, alone in the back room of the church. John bowed his head and said, "Preacher I don't know what to do anymore. I know it sounds absurd, but it is the truth."

John Bell declared, "I need help!"

The preacher tried to be reassuring. "John I've heard only gossip about this. I don't know what to make of it. Quite frankly, I don't believe you. All I can do is pray with you that this mystery solves itself."

The next day was Sunday. Most of the town was present at church. The Bell family, dressed in their finest clothes, sat near the front of the church. As the choir finished singing, everyone at the service sat up when the preacher took the pulpit.

"As many of you know, there is evil among us. Evil straight from hell. This evil is tormenting a well-respected family in our town, bringing them heartache and grief. Many of you are skeptical, as am I. But the fact remains that the Bell family is suffering through a difficult time right now. They need our support and prayers. And most importantly, they need God's love. Look to him. Pray to him. He is listen—"

Kate's unearthly voice exploded inside the church house, cutting the preacher off, "I am not evil."

The entire church gasped as one. Mrs. Johnston fainted dead away. The members of the congregation moved their lips in silent prayer. One elderly woman whispered loudly, "Who is that? Where is she?"

Kate the witch explained calmly, "Good folks, I do not come here to make enemies. Do not fear me."

Upon hearing the voice again, several women—and a couple of men—screamed. Most of the children started to cry. One terrified woman made a mad dash toward the door, but it slammed shut in her face.

The witch demanded, "And where do you think you are going?" The voice stopped the woman in her tracks. Kate continued, "I did not hear the preacher dismiss you. The service is not over; surely you are not leaving already?"

The woman slowly walked back to her seat, shaking like a leaf.

"Now that's better," the witch said in a calming voice.

The spellbound preacher gathered the courage to speak, "What have you come here for? This is a place of worship. You are not welcome here."

The witch giggled, a most horrible sound. "I am welcome wherever I go. I am not here to interrupt. I would simply like to attend your church service." The crowd murmured, but nobody moved. "Please continue, Mr. Preacher."

The whole congregation looked beseechingly at their pastor, knowing only God could help them now. The preacher stood quietly at the pulpit, then began to speak.

"If everyone will pull out their Bibles and turn to Isaiah chapter forty five, verse twenty-one." The congregation began to recite, "There is no God else beside me; A just God and a Savior; there is none beside me." As they read, the witch spoke with them. "Look unto me, and be saved, all the ends of the Earth: for I am God, and there is none else." They faltered to a halt.

"Amen!" came the voice.

The congregation was petrified. An evil spirit reciting the Bible? How could this be?

The preacher pulled out his hymnal. "Number one thirty-seven," he said. "Let's have a song to praise and worship our Savior, Jesus Christ."

He started alone, but other voices joined in raggedly until everyone was singing. A few smiles broke out as the hymn lifted people's spirits. Until Kate joined in. Her voice was pure and beautiful. One by one the congregation stops singing until Kate's was the only voice left. They were hypnotized by her intoxicating voice. The song ended, and all was silent. The preacher continued as if nothing was amiss. "Thank you, ladies and gentlemen." He glanced around, unsure how to proceed.

"Well, I think that is enough for today," the witch said. The church doors flew open. The congregation flooded out of the church; someone yanked open a window and crawled out. Everyone ran down to the road as if trying to get off church property. Back in the church, the tormented Bell family sat alone, still in shock. Finally they rose as one and headed back to their haunted home.

Later that day, Lucy Bell went about her chores even though she felt sick. Cleaning the kitchen took all her energy. Finally she collapsed in front of the fireplace to snap green beans. John Senior walked into the room and leaned against the mantle, weariness showing in his face. But he was concerned about Lucy. She seemed to be getting worse.

John asked lovingly of his wife, "Are you feeling any better, dear?" "I am still under the weather, but I am feeling a little better."

A knock at the front door interrupted the conversation. "Who could that be?" Lucy Bell asked. "A house call at this hour?"

Overhead, the witch's voice rang out, "Oh, it is the two town preachers together at your door."

John headed for the door, musing how strange it was to have a ghost for a butler. Her constant presence seemed to have diminished his fear. John opened the front door and found that the witch was correct. Standing before him were the pastor from the Bells's own Methodist church, Reverend Porter, and the reverend from the local Baptist church.

John made an effort to be cordial. He greeted his preacher. "Good evening, Reverend Porter. What can I do for you?"

"I am sorry to call on you so late, Mr. Bell, unannounced and all, but this is a matter of some urgency." Remembering his manners, he introduced his companion. "This is Reverend Lake from the Baptist church across town."The Reverend Lake said, "It is a pleasure to meet you." "Likewise," said John Bell. And the two men shook hands.

The Methodist preacher stammered around a bit and then said, "Mr. Bell, I rode over to Reverend Lake's church this afternoon. After the service this morning, I did not know quite what to make of the . . . disturbance, so I went to Reverend Lake for guidance, and well . . ."

The Reverend Lake interrupted, as it was apparent the Bells's pastor was having trouble explaining himself. "The truth be, Mr. Bell, I wanted to come see this for myself."

"Come in, gentlemen, if you dare." John Bell threw open the door and waved them inside. The two pastors entered slowly and uncertainly, looking around nervously, not knowing what to expect. John Bell saw the fear in their eyes. He wished for the hundredth time this ordeal was over.

"It is nice to see both of you again," Kate said from

nowhere. Both preachers spun around, searching wildly for the source of the voice.

This was Reverend Lake's first encounter, and he was astonished. He asked meekly, "Are you Kate?"

The witch proclaimed, "Yes I am."

The Reverend Lake had enough gumption to be polite. "I do not believe we have met," he said.

Kate replied, "We have not been properly introduced, Reverend Lake."

"Obviously, Kate, you are aware then of who I am?" the clergyman queried.

The witch laughed. "Of course I know who you are. I attended your service today."

"I did not see you there," the Reverend Lake countered. The Bells's preacher finally found his tongue. "That is impossible, Kate," he blustered. "You were at my church today. Our services took place at the same time on different sides of town."

Reverend Lake asked slyly. "If you were at my service, Kate, then what was my sermon about?"

Kate began talking, perfectly mimicking Reverend Lake's voice. "As prophesied by our Savior, our Lord will return to judge us one and all! The signs are out there! He is ready to return to his Father's creation, this place called Earth! Judgment day is coming! Are you prepared to follow Jesus? Are you prepared?"

The Reverend Lake was astounded. He couldn't believe what he was hearing: his own voice recited his sermon back to him by means of a witch.

Kate stopped and asked sweetly, "Reverend Lake, would you like me to continue?"

"No, no. I'm convinced. That was very impressive, Kate," Reverend Lake conceded.

"By the way sir, did you realize that you misquoted a passage today?" the witch asked coyly.

Reverend Lake drew himself up. He prided himself on his scriptural knowledge. "Kate, I think you are mistaken. I never misquote the Good Book," he said.

Reverend Porter agreed. "Kate, Reverend Lake has the entire Bible committed to memory. He knows it chapter and verse. I've never heard him so much as miss a word."

"Well, today, Reverend Lake," the witch explained, "You were speaking from the Book of Revelations, chapter twenty-one, verse three."

"Yes, that is correct."

"You said, 'And I heard a great voice out of the heavens saying, Behold, the tabernacle of God is with men, and he will dwell with them and they shall be his people, and God himself shall be them, and their God.' Isn't that correct?"

Reverend Lake said, "Yes, Kate, that is true. But that is the exact passage."

Kate said, "The verse says, 'God shall be with them.' You said, 'God shall be them.'"

Reverend Lake pulled his Bible from his pocket and began flipping through the pages. He stopped and ran his finger down the page. He blinked rapidly and closed his Bible.

"You are correct, Kate. May I shake your hand in congratulations?"

"Most certainly," Kate said. Reverend Lake stuck out his hand and held it there. Suddenly a presence shook his hand up and down. He turned white and yanked his hand away.

The entire Bell family had gathered around looking at the interaction between the pastors and the witch. Reverend Lake examined his hand, front and back. He got a calculating look and said, "Kate, may I shake your hand again?"

Sternly, the witch said, "Don't try and play those tricks

on me, Reverend. I am too smart for that. If I shake your hand again, you will try and catch me."

Reverend Lake protested, "Kate, I would do no such thing!" The witch snapped back, "You are a good man, but you are also a liar, sir."

With a glance at each other, the two preachers pulled out their Bibles. With the Good Book in one hand and a cross in the other, they fell to their knees and began to pray.

The witch mocked them. "So you two have come to exorcise me, have you?"

The two pastors continued to pray. Rising to their feet, they thrust their crosses into the air. The men began to preach simultaneously, each speaking over the other's voice.

Reverend Lake said, "In the name of that which is good and holy, leave this house." Reverend Porter joined in, "In the name of our gracious Lord, leave this family and let them live in peace!"

Reverend Lake stated, "Give them peace in the name of our Lord God the Savior."

Kate began to howl in pain. The preachers shouted scripture over her ear-piercing screams. Chairs fell over. Candles ignited themselves. The windows flew open and slammed themselves shut; the doors of the house did the same.

The preachers read together, "The Lord is my shepherd; I shall not want. He maketh me lie down in green pastures: He leadeth me beside the still waters. He restoreth my soul: he leadeth me in paths of righteousness for his name's sake. Yea, though I walk through the valley of the shadow of death, I will fear no evil: for thou art with me; thy rod and thy staff they comfort me."

The witch who called herself Kate bellowed out in agony, "Oh, please, no! I can feel the flames of hell burning at my feet! Please stop."

Reverend Lake declared, "It is working. The power of prayer conquers all." He continued with another scripture.

"For God so loved the world that He gave his only begotten Son, that whosoever believeth in Him should not perish, but have everlasting life."

Looking up from his Bible, the Reverend Lake commanded, "Cast yourself back into the burning flames of Hell where you belong."

Porter chimed in, "Lord strike down your sword upon this evil. Send her back to where she came from. Let her burn next to Lucifer."

The Reverend Lake shouted, "Let this spirit burn in eternity."

The witch screamed in horrifying pain, first in a human voice and then in the barks of dogs and the growls of wild animals. The Bells and the preachers covered their ears from the awful howls of agony. Finally, the witch went silent. Everyone looked around the room, straining to hear any sound at all.

John Bell was hopeful, "Has it left us?"

Pastor Porter offered hope. "I believe so." "Ha, ha, ha, ha, ha, ha, ha!" The witch's mocking laughter forced everyone to cover their ears again.

"You fools," Kate screamed. "I do not fear Hell. I existed long before Heaven or Hell. You preachers better go home before someone gets hurt!" Kate started to laugh wildly, loudly, enough to shake the windows in the house. The front door flew open in invitation.

Beaten down and broken-hearted, John Bell was almost crying as he escorted the two preachers to the door. Reverend Lake pulled a silver flask from his coat pocket and took a big swig, then wiped his brow. Cruelly disappointed that the exorcism had failed so miserably, the rest of the Bell family fled upstairs. They filed out on the balcony to watch the preachers, their last and best hope, prepare to depart.

"Well, gentlemen, as you can tell, my family is at their wits' end," John Bell said in discouragement.

Reverend Porter advised, "John, I think you should load your family up and move away from here until this thing is gone."

John Bell answered in an exasperated tone, "Preacher, don't you think we have already thought of that? The witch doesn't care. She says she will follow us anywhere. We're trapped, wherever we are."

The pastor said, "You believe she'll follow you anywhere you go?"

John Bell answered, "Without question. She has been mostly kind to everybody except for me. She used to torment my children, but she focuses only on me now."

The preacher said grimly, "Well, John, I don't know what to tell you. This is beyond anything I've ever imagined."

John Bell was resigned. "Thank you both, thank you so much." He shook their hands.

The men of the cloth mounted their horses and rode away, lighting their way with lanterns. John turned back to the house after watching the two preachers disappear in the night. The house had grown quiet. John Bell placed his injured hand on the front door. He bowed his head and said a silent prayer.

CHAPTER **14**

JOHN BELL HAD to force himself to enter his own house—but he thought about how his family needed him and crossed the threshold. He stood with his back to the door, hanging onto the doorknob.

"Kate?" John mustered the courage to whisper, needing to know if the witch was still present. "Kate, if you are still here, please answer me," he pleaded.

"So you think that you can get rid of me by exorcism, John Bell?" Kate laughed. Instead of her wall-rattling voice, she spoke in a low tone, almost as if she was trying not to disturb the rest of the family.

"What else can I do, Kate?" John asked.

"John Bell, answer me true. Did you really want those preachers to exorcise me, to destroy me?"

John Bell didn't answer her question directly. "Kate, you know you are not welcome in this house. You never were," he said.

He was rebuked with a slap to the face, so hard it knocked him to the floor.

"You will learn some respect, John Bell. I make the rules around here," the witch cackled. "This is no longer your house!"

John lay on the floor in dreadful pain. He coughed and gasped for air. He vomited up blood, which pooled on the floor. Blood began to flow from his bandaged hand, soaking the ragged cloth and dripping on the floor. He held the wounded hand up to examine it. His entire hand had turned blue, and large blue veins writhed down his wrist.

Kate laughed without remorse as John Bell, his body wracked by her torment, passed out on the floor.

Morning came, and John Bell awakened with a moan. He made his way upstairs to his bedroom where Lucy lay abed. She was sweating and had draped a wet washcloth over her forehead. John Senior sat on the bed next to her.

"Lucy, darling, try to drink some water," John said.

"Where are the children, John? I've got to make breakfast." Lucy looked groggily up at her husband, trying to rise from her sickbed.

"Betsy made us all some breakfast. Do not worry about a thing. I want you to rest today. Just stay in bed."

"John, I have chores to do," Lucy argued, trying to get out of bed.

"Oh, no you don't, Lucy," John said. "The children are going to take care of the chores. And I had Junior run to the doctor's house. You need to rest until he gets here this afternoon."

"Oh, John, don't get the doctor, it's just a little cold. It'll pass soon, I promise."

John wouldn't accept his wife's assurances. "No, no, no. You stay in that bed today, dear."

Lucy Bell fell back, exhausted. "Thank you, John," she sighed.

John kissed his wife lightly in the forehead and headed out to do his farm work. Lucy drowsed, hot with fever.

"Lucy," the voice of Kate came over from all around her.

"Don't worry, Lucy," the witch continued slowly and quietly, "I won't let anything happen to you."

Lucy said, "My husband John is taking care of me, and the doctor will be here in a little while."

Kate snorted. "John Bell can't even take care of himself, let alone a sick wife. And that doctor won't be able to find out what the problem is. But you are not to worry Lucy, your friend Kate is here to take care of you. Would you like some fruit?"

Lucy didn't understand and said, "Kate, there's no fruit in season. Where are we going to get fruit?"

Right over the bed, fresh grapes and apples appeared in the air and dropped to the bedspread. Lucy was shocked but couldn't resist the luscious fruit.

The witch sounded like someone's mother. "The fruit is good for you, Lucy," she said. "It's the only thing that will make you better."

Lucy didn't know what else to do, so she picked up a grape and put it in her mouth.

A smile washed over her face as she enjoyed the grapes. "Thank you, Kate, this is delicious."

The witch said sweetly, "Get some rest now, darling." Kate started to sing a beautiful song to soothe Lucy. The soft, sweet song quickly lulled Lucy Bell to sleep.

When he returned from summoning the doctor, Junior joined his Father in the field below the barn. Junior led the horse as his father walked behind, guiding the plow. Far in the distance they saw a plume of dust rising. As the wagon got closer, they saw it belonged to Kate Batts.

"Let me handle this," John Senior said, instructing John Junior to keep plowing.

Mrs. Batts had a man driving her wagon, chauffeuring her around. He pulled right up to John Bell Senior. Mrs. Batts looked down on him scornfully.

"What can I do for you, Mrs. Batts?" John asked, trying to avoid a fight.

"I've come to collect the rest of my money," Kate Batts almost shouted.

"I told you, madame, I've settled the matter with your husband. I paid him the agreed amount."

This infuriated Kate Batts to no end. "You tricked him into it. He has done gone plum crazy, and you manipulated him into it. The church will be after you—they know the truth. The preacher knows the truth. I won't stop, John Bell. I won't rest until I have my money."

John Bell couldn't help but laugh a bit at the bulldog of a woman. "Well, from the looks of it, you haven't rested in some time," he chuckled.

Kate Batts leaned down from the wagon seat and looked John straight in the eye. "Keep playing your little games, Bell. Go ahead, but none of this will stop until you pay me."

Kate Batts motioned for her chauffeur to drive on, and he slapped the reins against the horses.

John Bell headed back to his plow. His son was studying his father's face. He couldn't help it; he had to ask: "Father, did you trick old Mr. Batts into selling you that land?"

John Senior shook his head. "Of course not, son. You know me better than that. Don't let that crazy woman scare you."

As Kate Batts rode away, she pulled out her carrying case. Inside were hundreds of beautiful pins. She took a pin out of her jacket pocket and placed it carefully in the case.

About the time the doctor was due, John Senior headed for his front porch to wait. He was feverishly carving a wooden cross necklace. John smiled at the gentle old doctor when he arrived.

"Thank you, doctor, for coming to us. My wife's been feeling poorly."

The Bells were lucky the doctor was there at all. The rumors going around the community had scared everyone to death. But the doctor's sense of duty overcame his fear. "Yes, yes, please take me to my patient," he said. He was all eyes as they entered the house, looking around for the mysterious occupant he had heard so much about.

"I have heard some wild stories about this house, Mr. John Bell. Is there really a demon living here?"

John sighed. "We have been experiencing some family trouble recently, doctor. Don't be afraid," he said.

Reluctantly the doctor followed John up the stairs. They both heard Lucy and another woman talking. "Lucy, the doctor is here to see you," John Senior announced to his wife.

The doctor looked around the room wildly. "Mrs. Bell, I thought I heard another woman in here with you."

Kate the witch laughed. "I am right here in the room, Mr. Medicine Man."

The doctor clutched his black bag to his chest and backed up against the wall. "Don't be afraid you coward," Kate said. "Get over there and examine Lucy." The mortified doctor slowly peeled himself off of the wall where he had been doing a credible impression of wallpaper. He approached Lucy's bedside hesitantly. Opening his black medical bag, he pulled out a stethoscope, a mirror and a small reflex hammer. The doctor used the mirror to reflect candlelight down Lucy's throat. He inspected her lungs and heart with his stethoscope. He checked her reflexes and took her temperature.

The doctor turned to John Bell. "May I speak to you in the hallway a moment, sir?" he requested.

Outside the bedroom, the doctor took a deep breath and said, "Mr. Bell, I have been practicing medicine for a long time, and I have solved many perplexing problems. I simply don't know what is wrong with Lucy. She is obviously ill, but what is wrong I don't rightfully know. I suggest plenty of rest and fluids. I will be back later in the week to check in on her."

Back in the bedroom, Kate slowly and softly began to sing to Lucy. The doctor rolled his eyes at the unearthly singing, but he continued to talk to John Senior. "Lots of water and rest, Mr. Bell. That's all I can suggest," the doctor concluded. He then dashed down the stairs and ran out of the house.

John returned to his beloved Lucy's bedside and took her hand in his.

Lucy bravely responded to his caress. "Don't worry about me, John. I am feeling much better already."

"Lucy, the doctor says you're going to be okay. He'll be back later in the week to check on you," her husband informed her. He pulled the covers up to his wife's neck and patted her head.

Overhead came a loud rebuke from Kate, "You, sir, are a liar. The doctor does not know what's wrong with Lucy." Then the witch turned her attention to Lucy. "Don't believe his lies, Lucy."

John Bell Senior snapped, "Mind your business, Kate!"

The witch shouted back with anger, "Realize whom you are talking to, Bell!"

"Oh . . . ah . . . oh," John Senior started to scream and writhe in pain. He clutched frantically at his body. His tormented hand began to bleed again. He tore off the blood-soaked bandage and saw that the veins had turned black. His hand looked as if it was dying.

Lucy sat up in bed, cringing at the pain he was in. She pleaded, "What is it, John? What is it?"

"Lucy, it feels like pins and needles all over my body." John collapsed to the floor in agony.

Lucy begged of the air, "Please, stop it. Please, Kate." John quit screaming immediately. His eyes, closed tight against the pain, popped open in disbelief. The incredible pain was now completely gone, simply because his wife asked. John slowly collected himself and crawled up into bed with Lucy. They fell asleep together.

Far away in North Carolina, Professor Powell wrote a letter at a small cluttered desk. Books on witchcraft surrounded him. His letter read:

Dearest Betsy,
I am writing you this letter from North Carolina. While I'm here, I am doing some work for my family. I will be heading back to Tennessee in a few days and might be back before this letter reaches you. I want to tell you how I truly feel, but I am afraid of losing our wonderful friendship. I have not made my feeling for you abundantly clear.

When the letter from Professor Powell arrived a few weeks later, Betsy ran to her room and opened the letter with a large smile. She loved receiving mail. But slowly, the smile diminished as she read what the Professor wrote:

You are my prize student. You have always been. You are turning into a beautiful young woman whom I respect and admire.

Her smile turned swiftly to a frown as she read on.

I am in love with you, Betsy Bell. I will do everything in my power to make you my wife. I plan on moving North next year, where a good job awaits me. Please come with me. We will be forever happy.
                        Sincerely yours, Professor Powell

Betsy folded the letter, then shoved it into her pocket. Moments later, she heard her name yelled from outside her house. She ran over to the window and stuck her head out. It was Joshua.

"Come down and see me, Betsy Bell!" Joshua yelled up.

Betsy smiled and said, "I will be right down, Joshua." Betsy ran outside in a mad dash. The young couple joined hands and walked down the trail past the barn to the edge of the woods.

They found a soft spot near the riverbed. Betsy lay with her head on Joshua's stomach. A small waterfall gurgled, a refreshing and soothing sound.

"Betsy, do you remember when I asked you to be my wife last year?" Joshua asked.

Betsy looked up at him and replied, "Of course I do."

"Well, Betsy, I have been thinking some. You were right; we were too young then. But I think we are both older now, so I was hoping. . . ." Joshua's sentence stumbled to an end.

Betsy raised her head and stared Joshua in the eyes.

"Joshua? Are you asking me if I'll marry you?"

Joshua smiled shyly and replied, "Yeah, I guess I am asking that, aren't I? If it's still too soon, I understand. I don't want to put a lot of pressure on you. It's just—I'm just so much in love with you."

Betsy was silent for a second or so. The waterfall sparkled clean and clear in the sunlight. "Yes, I'll marry you, Joshua Gardner," she said.

Joshua's eyes flashed bright with excitement. "You mean it?"

"I do!" Betsy promised.

Joshua leaned down and gave her a soft kiss. "I love you, Betsy," he said.

"And I love you." The young couple kissed again.

"Mrs. Betsy Gardner. I like how that sounds," Betsy said. "So do I," Joshua said sweetly. The boy ran his hands through Betsy's hair as they kissed.

Meanwhile, back in the woods, Professor Powell was spying on the young couple. Just returned from North Carolina, he was on his way to visit Betsy Bell when he saw her and her beau head into the woods. He went into the woods and crept from tree to tree until he was close enough to hear their conversation. Soon, the Professor was enraged, and his long, thin face crumpled up in anger. Powell was unable to watch the young couple bill and coo, and he retreated to his buggy. All the way back, he smacked a fist against his open hand, over and over.

CHAPTER 15

THE TOWN OF Adams had a beehive buzz of gossip. In one home, two women darned socks and gossiped. The first lady asked, "Have you been down to the Bell house?"

"No, but I hear there is witchcraft and sinfulness going on."

"Lord help us, I hear it ain't no witchcraft. Them Bell boys have learned ventriloquism. They're doing all the talking, nothing more, nothing less."

"Is that so?" her friend remarked.

In another part of town, two men walked across the square.

"Son, it ain't no witch, for crying out loud," one insisted.

"What is it then, partner, a spook?"

"No, it's that daughter of theirs, Betsy. She's doing it."

"Say it ain't so," one protested.

"No, it's so!"

Betsy, in town for shopping, happened to cross the square at that moment.

"That's her right there. She's the one doing all of this," the man said. "She's reached the age where she wants attention. She's a good-looking little thing, which makes it doubly bad.

That explains why nobody else saw all those attacks on her."

On and on the whirlwind of gossip swirled around the small Southern town. It followed the Bells to church the next Sunday where they were greeted by much whispering and pointing as they took their seats up front.

A wife directed her husband's attention toward the pew where Kate Batts sat. In a whisper she explained, "People are saying ol' Kate Batts has put a spell on John Bell Senior for tricking her husband out of his land."

"The witch does call herself Kate," the husband pointed out.

"Exactly," the wife agreed. The point was settled in their minds.

The next day, at a local produce stand, the gossip spread.

". . . and I just rode by there the other day. You wouldn't believe what a spooky house it is. I'm on my way up North. Those Yankees ain't never heard anything the likes of what is happening in little old Adams, Tennessee. I can't wait to be the first to tell the tale. They won't even believe it," a man said excitedly.

"Oh, they'll believe it, all right. Yankees will believe anything. What I can't get over is how people around here can't stop talking about it. As for me, I think that schoolteacher is behind it," his friend said. As the tales got wilder, the stories spread more and more until almost everyone in town was involved in some way. The rumors about Professor Powell gained circulation, because he had let it slip that he had come to admire Betsy Bell.

In a corner of the square, one wizened woman held court. "That Professor is running for the legislature now. He's in love with that young girl, Betsy Bell. When he found out that John Bell Senior would not allow someone as old as he is to marry Betsy, the teacher vowed revenge. I hear he knows everything about the occult and witchcraft. He's got books on it and everything."

Her companion said, "I know for a fact that the Professor has wives in three different cities across the South." The crowd murmured at this revelation.

"He not only knows all about witchcraft," the little old lady added, "he practices it as well!"

"You don't say."

The ghost was also a hot topic. "She lives and sleeps in that cave near the Bell house," someone announced. But this was old news. "Oh yes, everyone knows that!" the old woman said scornfully.

On and on it went, worsening each day. Each tale grew more bizarre.

Behind the general store, two young men explained the occurrence to each other as they secretly shared a pipe of tobacco.

"That old John Bell built his house on top of an Indian burial ground. That's why he's got ghosts after him." His partner said, "He is a fool for doing that!"

"Oh yeah, now all those buried Indians want revenge. It ain't no witch at all. The Indians just want their land back. It's their land in the first place, ain't it?" he asked.

Even some of the Bells's neighbors, who should have known better, started their own hurtful rumors.

"John Senior has started to be mean to Lucy, treating her nasty-like," one reported.

"Well, if you ask me, the wife is behind it all. Why is the witch so kind to her all of a sudden—nursing her back and all. They say old Doc couldn't even tell what was wrong with Lucy Bell. Everyone knows that Lucy can't wait for John Senior to die so she can get her hands on all of that good farmland. It's the law in Tennessee, you know: The wife gets it all."

The neighbor snorted, "All of that is old news. General Andrew Jackson, Old Hickory hisself, has come down from out from Nashville to check it out for his own self."

"That right? Old Andrew came down himself?"

"That's correct. And you know what Old Hickory said?" Not waiting for the neighbor to guess, he blurted out the answer so no one could steal his thunder. "The General said he would rather face the entire British army again that to fight that ol' Bell Witch of Adams, Tennessee."

The only real truth to any of the gossip was that Andrew Jackson had indeed come to town. John Bell Senior used his son's connection to invite the General to his home to check out the story. The witch refused to appear, however, and Old Hickory made ready to leave without having seen anything.

"Thank you for coming, General Jackson," John Bell Senior declared. "I wish you could stay longer, sir; Lucy is preparing a delicious dinner."

"Thanks for the kindness, Mr. Bell." General Jackson said, warmly shaking John Bell's hand. With deep regret, he added, "I am just so sorry, sir, that I could not have been of more help in this matter."

John Bell shook his head and said, "Your coming here in itself was a great help, General. Please, take care on your trip back to the Hermitage and give my regards to Mrs. Rachel."

General Jackson rode off the Bell property, ramrod straight in the saddle. Distraught that the greatest man in Tennessee could be of no help, John Senior slowly walked back inside his home. He found Lucy and Betsy sitting in the parlor. As he joined them, Betsy said, "Father, Mother, I have something to tell you." Betsy looked at her parents with wide eyes.

"What is it, dear?" Lucy Bell looked up from her work.

Betsy cracked a slight smile showing her pleasure. "Joshua has asked for my hand in marriage."

Lucy put down her knitting materials and John sat on the sofa. Betsy continued, with a slight smile on her face, "It was just last week. With all that was going on and all, and all the visitors, I haven't had the opportunity to tell you the news."

"Well, Betsy," John Senior asked, finally having something to smile about. "What did you tell young Joshua?"

"I told Joshua Gardner that I would be his wife!" Betsy replied, beaming ear to ear.

John Senior was all smiles, too. "Joshua is a good boy, Betsy. You are going to be a happy young bride."

Lucy snuggled up to Betsy and declared, "Oh, Betsy, you are turning into such a fine young woman."

Betsy looked at each of her parents in turn. She asked, "So I have your approval?"

"Absolutely," Lucy stated, giving her daughter a hug. "Betsy," John Senior said, "Young Joshua asked me for my blessing nearly a year ago. I said I would be delighted to have him as my son-in-law."

The happy family moment was rudely interrupted. "Whore!" Kate shrieked her displeasure at the news that Betsy was going to marry Joshua. Then she said chidingly, "Betsy, Betsy, Betsy. So many secrets for such a young girl." The witch clucked her disapproval.

"Leave my daughter alone, Kate!" John Senior snapped.

An invisible hand smacked John across the face so hard it drew blood, and he cringed, doubled over in pain.

"Young Betsy, it would not be wise to marry that boy, Joshua," the witch declared.

Betsy Bell yelled back, "Why not?"

"Because I told you so!" Kate snarled.

"I am going to live my life like I want to live it, Kate!" Betsy yelled defiantly towards the ceiling.

"Oh you are?" the witch snapped back.

The witch grabbed Betsy's hair and lifted her off the ground. Betsy screamed hysterically as she tried to free her long locks, struggling helplessly in mid-air.

"Let my child alone!" John yelled as he ran over to Betsy and tried to pull her back to the floor.

WHACK. Kate smacked John away from his daughter.

THUMP. The witch released her hair and Betsy dropped to the floor crying.

"Please let us alone, Kate!" Betsy pleaded. "Please let us live in peace." She was sprawled on the floor, massaging her sore head.

The room grew silent. The family's happiness over Betsy's news was dimmed but not forgotten.

The next day Betsy went to find Joshua. He was pleased to see her, but the look on her face compelled him to ask, "What's wrong?"

"Nothing," Betsy fibbed. "Joshua, come walk with me for a while." She grabbed his hand and led him to the woods.

"Tell me what is wrong, Betsy," Joshua pleaded. "I know something is wrong. We are going to be married. You should be happy," he insisted.

Betsy squeezed Joshua's hand, pulling him to a stop. Betsy looked Joshua straight in the eye. "Joshua, I love you. You know I love you. Joshua, you know that, don't you?"

"Yes, Betsy, I know that. And I love you."

"Joshua, I don't know how to tell you this." Tears welled up in her eyes. "I can't marry you."

Joshua's face fell. "But why, Betsy?" he pleaded, his heart catching in his throat. He didn't really know what else to say except the first thing that popped into his head.

"Betsy, I am going to take over my father's farm. I will be able to support you and a family."

"Joshua, I know all of that," Betsy stared directly into Joshua's eyes. "It's not that!" Tears spilled down her cheeks.

Joshua took her by the shoulders with both hands and implored, "What is it then, Betsy?"

Betsy sobbed, "Joshua, it's Kate! That wretched old witch, she—she told me I can't marry you."

Stunned, Joshua's face turned crimson in anger. "She says what?! What does that . . ." Joshua searched for the right name to call Kate as he struggled with the news of Betsy's dilemma, ". . . thing have to do with our marriage? What does she know that we don't?" Joshua hugged Betsy to his chest.

"Betsy," Joshua continued, "Kate is a spirit, a witch, an apparition." He spoke slowly and deliberately. "What in the world does that . . . harpy have to do with us anyway?"

He had another idea. "Betsy, we'll move away. We'll move somewhere far away," Joshua proposed.

"Joshua, you don't understand." Betsy hugged him as hard as she could. "Kate has promised that if I marry you, I will never know a moment of peace as long as I live. Do you understand what that means?"

Betsy shook her head in despair at telling the man she loved she couldn't be with him. "That witch says she'll follow us if we move. We could never have children. She says she'll get to them and to their children. Look, Joshua, you don't know what it is like to live with that thing for twenty-four hours a day."

Betsy pulled away from Joshua just enough to look up into his eyes. "Joshua, you don't know what I am talking about because you haven't experienced it. You can't just say that we'll move away—we can't get away. Don't say we'll work our way through this because we can't." Betsy shook him by the arm to emphasize her last point. "And Joshua, what is more important is that I don't want to live through it, don't you see? I simply can't go through with our wedding knowing we'll be living through this nightmare over and over and over."

Joshua couldn't believe his ears. Betsy Bell was the smartest person he knew. He believed down deep that they could beat that old witch Kate. They were meant to be together, he thought; they had been meant to be together since they were children.

Joshua stumbled for something to say. "Kate's bluffing, Betsy. Please don't listen to her," Joshua begged. He grabbed Betsy by the waist and pulled her to him. "We love each other, Betsy," Joshua whispered. Then he looked into Betsy's eyes and implored, "Don't we? Don't we love each other, Betsy?"

"Of course we do, Joshua." Betsy admitted. "Yes, we do love each other, but. . . ."

"But what, Betsy?" Joshua pleaded. "Betsy, I simply don't know what I will do if I can't have you!" Tears welled up in Joshua's eyes as well.

Betsy tried to answer but she couldn't speak through her tears. She pulled away from Joshua, touched her hand to his cheek. "Please Joshua . . . I'm sorry," she cried and ran off through the woods away from him.

Joshua grabbed his head in agony and yelled out, "Please don't you do this to us, Betsy Bell!"

That night, what descended on Betsy was darker than dark. She could see no good in the world. She couldn't have the man she loved. She couldn't be with the family she loved because of the evil that had invaded her life. She didn't understand why God had forsaken her family so.

Betsy sat in her room alone, with a sole candle flickering, providing only a bit of light. Tears poured down her face. When Betsy thought of all the things that were wrong in her life, her chest began to heave and she had trouble catching her breath.

Kate called out to Betsy, "Betsy dear?"

Betsy refused to respond, instead trying to hold her tears back. She stared at the candle flame to focus her mind.

The witch spoke again to Betsy in a sweet voice. "Betsy dear? Betsy dear," Kate repeated. "Dear, are you okay?" Betsy refused to speak and ignored Kate instead.

"Betsy, I know what you did today was difficult. One day you will thank mc, Betsy dear. You did the right thing," Kate continued in a soothing voice.

"Betsy, do you need anything?" the witch asked. Betsy steadfastly refused to speak; she cried and stared at the flickering candle flame and thought only of Joshua.

"Please talk to me, Betsy. I only want what is best for you, dear. Betsy, don't be sad," the witch cooed. Betsy said nothing, and the ghost fell silent.

The next day at the Bell house, Lucy was cutting vegetables for the family meal when she heard a knock at the door. It was Professor Powell, holding a dozen beautiful roses.

"Good day, Mrs. Bell," the tall Professor said with a bow.

"Why, Professor Powell, what a nice surprise," Lucy said. "What can I do for you, Professor?"

"I'm sorry to bother you, but I have written some letters to Betsy and she has not responded. I thought I'd take up the matter in person."

Mrs. Bell smiled uncertainly at the Professor and declared, "Well, Professor, come in and have a seat. I'll go fetch Betsy. I'm sure she will be delighted to see you."

Lucy led the Professor to the parlor and showed him to a seat. She walked to the stairwell and called up, "Darling, you have company."

Betsy came around the corner asking, "Who . . .?" She stopped short when she saw her visitor. "Why, Professor Powell, what are you doing here?" The Professor stood up, offered her the bouquet. "Betsy, my dear. These are for you." Betsy smelled the flowers and smiled at her teacher. "Why thank you, Professor," she said. "But tell me, to what do I owe this visit and these flowers?"

"Betsy, I wrote you letters but you never responded. Why not?" the Professor asked, looking puzzled. Then with a look of hope, he added, "Betsy, did you not get them then?"

Betsy studied her flowers and then looked down to the floor. "Yes, Professor, I received your letters. I did not know how to answer then, and I don't know now. Things are a bit confusing— I broke up with Joshua only yesterday."

The Professor walked over to hug the saddened girl. Betsy was uncomfortable, almost frightened in his long, thin arms.

Back in the kitchen, Lucy wondered about the Professor's visit when she heard another knock at the door. She opened it to find Joshua Gardner on the porch, also armed with a beautiful bouquet of flowers.

"Hello, Mrs. Bell, is Betsy in?" Joshua asked.

Lucy smiled at the boy. "Hi, Joshua, come on in. She is in the parlor visiting with Professor Powell."

"Professor Powell is here?"

"Yes, Joshua. I am sorry about everything that has happened between you and Betsy. John and I really like you. We're sure sorry how this has turned out."

Joshua smiled back. "Thank you, Mrs. Bell. Hopefully it is not over with yet."

Lucy showed him to the parlor. "Lucy, dear," she said as they walked in, "you have another guest."

They both stopped short as they saw the Professor holding Betsy. From Joshua's point of view, it appeared as if Betsy was enjoying the hug.

Joshua threw down his bouquet of flowers and snapped, "Now I see how it is."

The Professor let go of Betsy, who sprung away then stood frozen when she saw Joshua.

"So it was the witch that told you to break up with me, was it? Some witch," he said, looking the Professor up and down.

Betsy shook her head, saying, "Joshua, it's not what you think. The Professor just came by. . ." She didn't finish her sentence because Joshua just noticed the flowers that the Professor brought.

Joshua spat out, "It looks like he just came by to give you flowers."

"Yes, Joshua, but no, that's not it." Betsy protested to no avail. Joshua kicked his flowers as he stormed out of the Bell house. Betsy started to run out after him, yelling "Joshua!"

Professor Powell halted her by grabbing her arm. "Betsy, let the boy go. He needs some time to think. He's just a young boy, after all." The Professor tugged her closer. "Go and see him tomorrow night, after he's had some time."

Betsy tried to protest, but the bony teacher pulled her closer. "Trust me, young Betsy. If you follow Joshua now, it'll turn into one big argument. Betsy, I was a young man once too. I know how they think." The Professor smiled through his crooked teeth. "You're beautiful, young Betsy," he murmured. The girl pushed him away in horror. "Go away, I hate you," she shouted. She ran upstairs and threw herself on the bed, where she cried herself to sleep.

Down the road a ways, Joshua was asleep as well. A wispy film of fog floated over his bed and slowly materialized into the form of Betsy dressed in all white. "Betsy" lifted the covers and crawled into bed beside Joshua. She put an arm around him and pulled him close. He was half asleep and murmured, settling into her arms.

"Can I stay here with you tonight, Joshua?" the witch whispered in Betsy's voice.

In a dream-like trance, Joshua said, "Yes, Betsy. But darling, be very, very quiet. We would not want my father to wake up."

Kate caressed him, and Joshua responded with pleasure. She scratched his chest with her nails and blood trickled down his belly. Joshua's eyes sprung open in shock. The young man turned to find emptiness next to him in bed. His chest burned. He sat up and ripped the blankets off his chest in terror. Blood was pooling in his bed.

The temperature in the room suddenly plummeted. Joshua pulled the blanket up because he was freezing. His breath was visible with each panting breath he took.

Kate began to laugh hysterically.

"The only person you will be sleeping with, Joshua Gardner, is . . . me!" Kate howled. The witch relished the fear she instilled in the young man.

Joshua suddenly twisted his face up. He covered his nose, almost gagging. The most foul stench he had ever experienced overwhelmed the room. "Joshua, don't you want me now?" Kate cackled. Joshua vomited from the stench, then collapsed to the floor, covered in the blood-soaked bed clothing. He broke down and cried.

He lay on the floor frozen in terror until the sun crept up and a heartwarming ray of light illuminated Joshua's room. He crawled feebly into his bed and fell deeply asleep.

At the Bell house, the sun's arrival dispersed the uncertainty of the darkness. Williams woke up first and carried his father's boots to him. They had a difficult journey ahead of them. "Here, Father, I've come to give you a hand," Williams said as he helped his father dress, tying his boots for him.

"Thank you, son. Hand me that glass of water, please."

SPLAT. Kate slapped the glass away from him and it shattered, splashing water everywhere.

John sighed. "Forget the water, Williams," he said. "Can you give me a hand?"

John Senior steadfastly tried to stand, needing the strength of his son to be able to do so. Williams grimaced as he actually heard his father's bones creak and crack. Williams asked his father, "Are you ready for this?"

John Senior looked at his son and said, "I have to be." Williams helped his father down the stairs. They made their way out on the porch and into the waiting wagon. Williams grabbed the reins and drove them down the road.

They drove past the woods to their church just outside of Adams. When they arrived, Williams repeated his actions in reverse. He steadied the horse, and then helped his father down from the wagon. Williams led John Senior carefully up the steps into the church.

A group of five church elders sat at the front of the church. Williams helped his father to a chair in front of the men. John was coughing violently.

The group began to discuss at length the occurrences of the past few weeks. John Senior listened as long as he could before he interrupted. "Gentlemen. I have already said my piece, and I do not have the strength to repeat it. I paid Mr. Batts the amount we agreed upon."

The preacher said, "Mr. Bell, I am sympathetic to your troubles. I know you are ill, but by not responding to our questions, we have no choice but to assume you are guilty of the charge against you."

John Senior scowled. "I am guilty of making an intelligent business transaction with a neighbor. But that is all I am guilty of," he protested.

The preacher continued his argument. "Mr. Bell, the church has evidence and witnesses saying you coerced Mr. Batts into the agreement. If you do not wish to respond to this evidence, we. . ." He stopped as a look of disgust came over John Bell's face. He interrupted the preacher, "To hell with your evidence and your witnesses. In fact, to hell with this church."

The group of men stared at each other, and then at John Bell, in disbelief. John Senior stood his ground and glowered back at the panel of his judges.

"From this day forward, Mr. Bell, you and your family are no longer members of this religious affiliation. It will be noted that you have made blasphemous remarks on your final day as a member of this church," the preacher said, shaking his finger in John Bell's face.

John Bell coughed until he was red in the face. Then he retorted, "Gentlemen, let the record show that I made blasphemous remarks to each and every one of you!" With that, John Bell hobbled out of the church supported by his son.

Inside the church, the preacher motioned to the secretary taking the minutes of the meeting. "John Bell Senior is officially ex-communicated from this church on this day."

Outside, Williams helped his violently ill father get back into the wagon. Williams took the reins and they set off for home. "Williams," John Senior said, between wheezes and coughing spells.

"Yes, Father?" Williams replied, a worried expression on his face.

"Williams, I know that was hard for you to watch. One day you will understand why I acted like that. Sometimes you just have to stand up for yourself. You can't let others trample all over you. You understand, Williams?" Williams nodded. John began to cough violently, then he collapsed and fell off the wagon.

CHAPTER 16

"FATHER," WILLIAMS SCREAMED as he leaped off the wagon and grabbed John Senior, who was lying on the ground motionless. Williams managed to get his limp body back into the wagon. Then he drove directly home as fast as he could.

As he pulled in the gate, Lucy and Betsy came running out and helped get John Senior into the house and up to his room. Lucy sent Williams back to town to summon the doctor.

Later that afternoon, the doctor finally arrived. He examined John Senior as Lucy held her husband's hand. The doctor looked around the room, then nodded his head and murmured to himself a bit. He said to the family, "This is a difficult case. But Mr. Bell should be okay if he gets ample rest and lots of water. Rest is the key. With good luck, he will be well within a week or so."

Lucy was relieved to hear that. She left her husband's side to hug the doctor. "Thank you, Doctor. " "Lucy," the physician warned, "don't let him get out of bed. He is stubborn, I know. However, you must make sure he rests. Most of all, make sure he sleeps."

"Okay, Doctor." Lucy promised.

"Okay, children. Junior, Betsy and Williams, let's follow

the doctor's orders. Let father get some rest." Junior and Betsy followed the physician out of the room.

Williams asked, "Mother, can I stay with Father? In case he needs anything. I promise to make him stay in the bed and I will be quiet and not wake him."

"Okay, Williams," Lucy said, "but let Father sleep."

"I will, Mother, I promise." Williams said.

Williams pulled up a chair next to his father's bed and tucked the blankets a little tighter. John Senior slumbered away. It had been a long, arduous day for his son, and he soon found himself falling asleep. That was when Kate renewed her mission of torturing John Bell Senior. She started by whispering to him in Lucy's voice, "Sleep, John. You need your sleep, John. Sleep. . . ." Then slowly, carefully the witch began to lift John off the bed, straight up in the air. John woke up in the middle of the air and screamed. Williams awoke with a start. He was horrified to see his father suspended over the bed.

"Father!" Williams screamed in terror.

Kate dropped John directly onto the wooden floor with a horrific crash. John was so injured from the drop of eight feet that he could hardly raise his head. He began to cough violently again, so harshly that his son had to hold him for a moment. Then Williams helped John back into bed.

Kate started whispering into John's ear. "Now go back to sleep! You need your sleep." Williams swore that this time he would stay awake to protect his father from the witch.

The next day, Betsy and Lucy resumed their work out in the garden. After a while, Betsy looked up from tending the green beans and asked, "Mother, can I take one of the horses?"

"Where do you need to go?" Lucy asked her young daughter.

"I need to go over to Joshua's. I haven't seen him since he

saw me with Professor Powell. The more I think about it, I need to talk to him about everything, to explain everything to him."

Lucy looked at her daughter with sympathy. She said, "You don't know, Betsy?"

Betsy shook her head and asked, "Know what?"

"Betsy dear, I'm sorry. Joshua left earlier this week. He went down to New Orleans and got a job down there. After the whole thing with you and. . . ." Lucy's voice trailed off.

"Mother, what?" Betsy begged.

"After the you broke up with him and then the whole thing with Professor Powell, I just guess that Joshua felt like there was nothing for him in Adams anymore."

Betsy's eyes filled with tears and she started to tremble. "Mother, you're lying!" she cried in disbelief.

"Betsy, darling, I wish I were," Lucy replied, stroking her daughter's hand with compassion. She pulled her close and whispered, "I'm sorry."

Betsy was so overwhelmed with emotion that she pushed her mother away and ran inside the house.

Meanwhile, inside the house, John Senior said, "Williams, help me to that chair, will you?"

Williams smiled as he helped his father out of the bed and into the chair. "Are you feeling better, Father?" he asked.

"Williams, I just need to rest here for a while."

The two heard liquid dripping on the floor. At their feet was a puddle of blood. More blood was oozing from the bandage on John Bell's hand. He unwrapped the dressing to examine the wound. The veins were distended, horribly discolored, and his hand looked as if it was going to rot off.

"This cut is just not going to heal," John declared. He wrapped the wound tighter with a fresh dressing.

"Let's get you back into the bed," Williams said.

His father refused.

"Williams, while I am up, I want to go out and check on the animals."

Williams shook his head. "Not today, Father. Junior is taking care of the farm for you."

"Williams, be a good son. I can't lie in this bed forever." Williams didn't want to start a fight. He wrapped an arm around his father and helped him downstairs and out of the house.

It was a beautiful Tennessee afternoon. Williams and his father tried to make small talk about the weather, avoiding the horrible circumstances that overwhelmed their family. The distraught father, supported by his loving son, headed toward the barn.

Unbeknownst to them, John Senior's shoelaces were slowly coming untied as they crossed the barnyard. John tripped over them, and Williams, ever the dutiful son, rushed to his father's aid.

"I thought I tied those shoestrings tight," Williams declared. "Let me try again." As he bent to tie the laces, the witch hurled the shoes thirty feet away.

John Senior got up as fast as he could and approached his shoes.

Kate snarled, "Where do you think you're going Bell?" The witch gave her high-pitched cackle that the Bell family knew too well. "You need to be in bed!"

Kate then knocked John off of his feet; he fell to the hard red clay and grimaced in horrific pain. Williams rushed to help his dad and saw something he had never, ever seen before: John Bell was crying like a child. He had been through so much that he did not care that his son saw him sob and heave like a girl.

"Williams, my dear boy," John cried through his agony, "I hate you to see this."

Williams shook his head as he tried to get his father off

the ground. "That's okay, Father," Williams assured. He, too, had to fight back tears as he watched the man he respected so much in such agony. John Senior again struggled to his feet with his son's help. And as much as he regretted saying it, he admitted something that he never thought he would say: "Williams, I don't know how much more I can take of this."

Williams brushed the tears from his father's face and lifted him on his shoulder. "Don't say such things, Father. Let's get you back into bed. Tomorrow will be a better day." As they struggled back into the house, Kate laughed her despicable cackle. She continued throughout the night. Over and over Kate's wicked laughter echoed over the Bell farm, reflecting the evil joy she obtained from torturing John Bell .

Later that night, the Bell family finally managed to fall asleep, in spite of the witch's unending laughter and their own tormented thoughts. All slumbered except young Williams, who would not leave his father's side. Williams kept a small candle lit on the floor at John Senior's bedside and watched his father sleep. The candle was flickering, amplifying the horrific sight of John Bell's skeletal body. Determined as Williams was, and try as he might to remain vigilant, sleep was overtaking him. Williams's head bobbed and weaved, jerked and ducked, and finally, the weary youngster went to sleep.

Now that the entire household slept, a light evening breeze drifted through the bedroom window where John and Williams rested. Williams's candle was snuffed out by the menacing whiff of night air. The unmistakable smell of the extinguished candle permeated every corner of the room. John Senior awoke to complete darkness. He looked over and saw the dim outline of his loyal son Williams. John Senior tried to call out to his son, but he was too weak to make a sound.

He tried again. "Williams. . . ." John Senior was finally able to gasp.

His son was so soundly asleep, he was unable to hear his father's desperate voice. John looked past his son toward the door. It began to creak slowly open, letting a bit of candlelight invade the room. Lucy glided in from the hallway. As sick as he was, John Senior was able to manage a slight smile at the sight of his beautiful wife. She was wearing an elegant white dress, her long locks piled on her head and held in place by two gorgeous brown combs. Glowing radiantly, she approached John's bedside as gracefully as any woman John had ever seen.

"Lucy, darling?" John was able to say, almost too quietly to hear.

His wife was carrying a clear bottle of liquid so blue it almost glowed in the night. Lucy came to the bedside, taking care not to awaken Williams. She leaned over the bed and kissed her husband on the forehead.

"It's only me, John," Lucy whispered.

"Lucy," John protested, "You're not well; you should be asleep like the doctor says." Lucy pressed her finger to his lips.

"Shhhhh! John. We don't want to wake anyone," she whispered. Lucy nodded toward Williams, sound asleep just a couple of feet away. John managed to nod in agreement. Lucy extended the bottle of effervescent blue liquid to her husband. "Drink this, John," Lucy ordered her husband, holding the bottle to his lips. The mesmerizing liquid glistened in a beam of moonlight that had filtered into the room through a crack in the curtains.

John couldn't take his eyes off the glistening concoction. Suddenly, his face turned up into a frown, and he turned his nose away.

"Oh Lord, Lucy," John objected. "That smells awful."

"John, it will help you get well. Please drink it, for the good of the family."

Lucy smiled and lifted her husband's head with one hand while she brought the bottle to John's mouth. She poured the blue concoction into his mouth. John shut his eyes and swallowed hard. Lucy then kissed him lightly on the lips.

After he choked the liquid down, John opened his eyes and looked to his wife. To his horror, Lucy's eyes turned blood red. He blinked in disbelief. When he looked again, Lucy looked completely normal. So fleeting was the transformation that John thought he had suffered a hallucination.

"Sleep now, John. Sleep forever," Lucy purred. John Bell's eye lids grew heavy, flickering open and shut. Then they closed. Forever.

The empty crystal bottle floated across the bed, supported by an unseen hand. It landed on John's bedside table. Then the door to the bedroom opened and closed by itself. John Bell lay completely motionless, drawing not a single breath. Williams slept deeply, slumped over in the chair by his father's bed.

Only the normal sounds of the night—crickets and owls and the rustling wind—enveloped the Bell farmhouse. John Bell's family slept peacefully, at last.

CHAPTER 17

JOHN BELL'S BODY lay peacefully in his pine casket, dressed in his favorite Sunday suit with a bright pink rose inserted in the lapel. The Bell family and half of the countryside turned out for the funeral. The ceremony was held in the parlor at the Bell family home. The church held fast to John's excommunication, even after his death.

After the funeral, the pallbearers closed the simple casket and loaded it onto a horse-driven caisson for travel to the gravesite. Dozens of folks arrived by horse, wagons and carriages to pay their final respects. Slowly and inexorably the casket lowered into the hole dug out of the Tennessee dirt. The sweet sounds of *Amazing Grace* flew over the crowd. It was John Bell's favorite hymn, and his daughter, Betsy, sang it beautifully. Betsy's tears flowed freely as she reached her father's favorite lines.

> "When we've been there ten thousand years, bright shining as the sun, we've no less days, to sing God's praise, than when we'd first begun!"

The sweet hymn stirred fond memories, joyful remembrance of times past, and caused John Bell's eyes to flicker open. He was confused at first. He was in the dark. It was so hot and stuffy. A curious THUD THUD THUD sounded from just above his face.

Up above, Junior and Williams shovelled the red clay over their father's casket as quickly as they could. Only the Bell sons filled the grave. This final task gave them closure and freed them to mourn their dead father. The bereaved boys wiped away tears with their white shirtsleeves and continued to hurl dirt in the hole.

"John, John Bell. . . ." Kate's voice filtered through the wood that surrounded him. The witch's words jolted John wide awake.

"Time to wake up now," the witch laughed softly. "I told you I would get you, John Bell!"

Slowly the horror of his plight began to dawn on John Bell Senior. His fingertips explored the silk surrounding him; he measured out the size of his enclosure. The blood drained from his face as he realized he had been buried alive!

"Help! Help!" John screamed at the top of his lungs. He was thinking feverishly, trying to remember what happened. He must have been deceived; that wasn't Lucy, it was that witch, Kate! John Senior visualized the blue liquid that he drank, understanding the terrible lie he had swallowed.

"Help! Help!" John screamed again and again, clawing in panic at the top of the casket lid. He tried to push it open, but it was bolted shut, and by now, covered with a thick layer of red clay dirt. John realized that there was not much air in the box. The thought made him gasp for breath. His chest heaved as the oxygen level grew low. It was becoming a struggle to stay alive.

Standing around the grave was everyone that John Bell Senior loved. Betsy, Lucy, Williams, and Junior mourned his passing. Professor Powell held onto Betsy, stroking her as she cried uncontrollably. The townspeople paid their final respects. James Johnston began to sing an old Scottish hymn.

Suddenly Kate, the evil witch, started to laugh, softly at first, almost drowned out by the thud of dirt on the casket and the lone voice singing. Her evil cackle grew louder until everyone could hear her.

James Johnston faltered at first, then continued singing louder and louder, defying Kate to drown him out. His simple tenor penetrated to the casket, where John Senior struggled again and again to escape. He pounded on the lid to no avail. John Senior pushed until his arms were bruised, then hammered with his fist until his knuckles bled. With what little air remained, he screamed, "Help! You've buried me alive! You've buried me alive!" Tears of terror rolled down the man's cheeks as he realized no one could hear him.

He was frantic now. He knew he didn't have much time. "I am alive!" he screamed. He scrabbled at the lid until his fingernails ripped out.

Kate's grotesque laughter finally drowned out James Johnston's proud singing. The crowd of family, friends and townsfolk could take no more and fled the graveyard.

Only John Junior and Williams Bell remained. The witch wouldn't even allow them a moment of peace with their father. Soon, fear and despair overcame the two boys and they turned away from their father's grave.

CHAPTER **18**

1943

SETH, ANDREW AND Mary Jane sat mesmerized in the front pew of the old church. The fire had dwindled to embers, and the old church was icy cold. Katherine was energized by her performance, delighted to impart the story of the Bell Witch in such a horrifying manner. She felt magnificent.

But the children's faces told a different story. Mary Jane had tears in her eyes. Seth moved as close to her as he could, but he kept a little distance between them so the young girl didn't feel his knees knocking in fear. Andrew was on the verge of either vomiting or running screaming out of the old church; both were a distinct possibility.

Katherine proudly surveyed her three pupils and saw how upset they were. But she didn't care. In her view she had given a fair account of those long-ago events. "Remember, we're going to discuss what the story means," Katherine said. She thought that by reminding them of the drama class—the reason they were here—it would help bring them back to reality.

"Did John Bell Senior deserve his treatment for cheating

poor old Kate Batts out of the money for the land?" Katherine asked. "Or do you believe it was really all a hoax?"

"You mean they really buried him alive?" Seth asked, eyes as wide as saucers.

CLAP CLAP CLAP came the sound of a single pair of hands. The three youngsters' heads jerked around to see who was applauding. "Daddy!" Mary Jane shouted out delightfully; running to join her father, Jake. Seth and Andrew left their seats and joined Mary Jane and Jake Bell.

"The story never changes, does it, Kate?" Jake Bell asked in a hard voice.

"The name is Katherine!" the young teacher snapped. Upon seeing Jake Bell, Katherine's plain clothes instantly transformed into flamboyant purple robes, trimmed with gold, ermine and sable, regalia born of a place and era far removed from the Smoky Mountains of Tennessee.

The children gasped when they witnessed the sudden physical transformation of their schoolteacher. The fire that had died in the stone fireplace roared back to life with a vengeance. Strangely, it seemed to emit no heat; indeed, the building was getting colder and colder.

"John cheats the old woman and deserves to be slowly tortured and then deliberately murdered. Is that your idea of justice?" Jake Bell asked.

"Well, it's the truth, John," Katherine snapped as she settled the long flowing robes around her. Rearranging her clothes revealed a tattoo on her neck, a garish image of two serpents in a writhing embrace.

"Have you forgotten? My name is Jake!" the man asked.

Katherine snarled as she mounted the stage of the old church. The physical transformation from sweet young schoolteacher into frightening vixen was almost complete. Andrew, Seth and Mary Jane cowered behind Jake Bell.

"John, Jake, what is the difference, anyway?" Katherine exploded with anger. "With apologies to Shakespeare, a Bell is a Bell is a Bell. That's what I've always said," Katherine stated. "Even that young daughter of yours, the great-great-great-granddaughter of John Bell, realized the resemblance of this story to the ancient Roman and Greek tragedies," Katherine continued.

"And what is that, Katherine?" Jake asked. Katherine was extremely agitated, so angry she began trembling uncontrollably. At the top of her voice, she shouted, "The man stole! And he was punished for his sin!"

Mary Jane cried out, "Is that what the big secret was about!" She still clung to her father. "This has to do with my own family?"

Jake Bell looked down at his frightened daughter and hugged her tight. "Yes, dear, it does, but you don't understand it all. Your great-great-great-grandfather was a good man. He was no thief."

"Liar!" Katherine snapped angrily. Jake Bell crossed his arms on his chest and laughed. "That's what you say, Kate! You and yours have always said that, down through the ages. If someone won't bow down to you and your brother, then you make false accusations and take everything from them, the people they love, their home, their faith and finally their lives."

He looked down at Seth, Andrew and Mary Jane, who had their arms wrapped around him. "You may scare these children, Kate or Katherine, whatever you call yourself. But you don't scare me!"

"Oh, really?" Katherine retorted. "So you're not afraid of me?" she asked mockingly. Jake shoved the children behind him to protect them.

Katherine's raven dark hair first started to waft up toward the rafters, blown by an unseen wind. Then her purple robe began to flap wildly. Katherine floated off the stage, her hands raised to the church's rafters. The frightened group could not believe the physical transformation occurring right in front of their very eyes.

Katherine's eyes rolled back in her head and she opened her mouth unnaturally wide, making a hissing sound almost too low to hear. This brought a wave of bats down from the rafters of the old church. Scores of the black bats flew around crazily, controlled by Katherine's black magic. The bats swirled around her.

Mary Jane clung to her father even tighter. Her scalp where the bat had bitten her started to bleed again. Katherine began flying around the rotting old church, approaching the rafters as she moved ever higher. The big room grew colder still, and the children's heaving breaths turned into fog, condensing into icicles on their clothing.

"So what is the meaning of all of this horror spreading down throughout the years?" Jake Bell shouted. "Is it power? Is it money? Revenge? Why follow us up here to these beautiful mountains?"

"Silence, you mortal. To answer your question, Bell, it is all of it!" came the explosive response. The witch hovered directly over them, looking down at three frightened children and one defiant man.

The apparition began to grow. Perhaps it was the group's fear, or because the moment of reckoning was approaching, but the witch's power increased exponentially. More bats, devils of the night, appeared from nowhere, circling and diving, baring their razor-sharp teeth. The witch gestured at the frightened group, and the bats began to attack. As Jake and the children tried to protect themselves, the church door banged open with a thundering echo. In walked Rellie, Violla and Rhode. Rellie shouted, "Jake, Rhode said you needed help, so here we are!"

His slicked-back hair almost stood on end when he saw the eight-foot monster soaring overhead.

"Who in the devil are you? Rellie asked.

The apparition flew straight at him and shouted, "I am the Bell Witch!"

"We know who you are, Kate!" came the slight but determined voice of the white-haired Rhode. Her quiet manner appeared to make the Bell Witch's face explode into crimson anger. Hatred flashed from Kate's eyes like lightning bolts. She was now ten feet tall, her immense body filling the rafters of the church. The witch vomited forth more ultrasonic noise, igniting the black bats in a fury.

"So soon we meet again, witch," Rhode stated. She walked right up to the enormous apparition. The church began to shake. An evil wind stirred Rhode's white hair.

Jake Bell was first to understand. "You two really know each other?"

Rhode nodded in acknowledgment, giving Jake an "I told you so" look. Then Rhode said, "Mr. Bell, outlandish as it seems, this old witch and I go back a long, long time."

"But you weren't there to help old John Bell, were you, Rhode, my sweetie?" Kate bellowed.

"Oh, no, I was not there," Rhode acknowledged. "I was needed to fight your brother! But, that was then. I am here now!" Rhode declared, not budging an inch.

Kate exploded in anger. "Rhode, keep my brother, the master, out of this!" Smirking at the huge monster overhead, Rhode snorted in disgust. "The master?" She laughed. "Your brother is not the master!"

The witch's red eyes grew large with hatred for her nemesis, Rhode. For these two, this confrontation had been played out many times over many eons.

Rhode began to quote scripture rapidly and rhythmically. And very much to the chagrin of the witch, the power of the Word began to wound Kate. Rhode knew the words of the Bible that would cut the deepest and inflict the most damage. Her rendition of the Word was strong enough to destroy Kate, perhaps for eternity. The preachers who had tried to help John Bell so long ago were weak and human. Thus, they were unable to exorcise the demon. But Rhode was pure, and her words were powerful.

With each Bible verse, a maelstrom of wind began to swirl around the witch. Dust and debris, papers and leaves, formed a funnel cloud around the demon. The bats swirled erratically, flying against the whirlwind that encircled Kate.

She was howling in anguish—the witch was being wounded as Rhode read parts of the book of Revelation. Kate began to diminish in size. The witch threw her hands over her ears and screamed, "Stop it. I can't stand this. I'll leave. I'll go away. I promise I will go away for a long time . . . forever, if you want me to, Rhode! You win, you win." She peeked at Rhode out of the corner of her eye to see if the mountain woman was falling for her lies.

"Baloney!" Rhode shouted, then continued reciting scripture. Kate was writhing in pain and dwindling in size. The wounded witch frantically directed the bats to attack. The small black soldiers from Hell dive-bombed Rhode again and again. The dark-winged villains were ruthless and unrelenting, slashing every inch of Rhode's exposed skin. Despite the barrage of razor-sharp teeth, Rhode didn't flinch, though the wounds must have hurt deeply.

She knew it was time. She shouted out at the top of her lungs, "Now, Rellie, now, Violla!!" Rhode shouted as the wind raged on and the bats slashed.

"You fight fire with . . . fire!" Rhode shouted, blood staining her white hair. Rhode was staring Kate directly in the eyes, not daring to glance away from the evil witch lest she escape. Violla and Rellie were petrified with fright, not remembering what they had planned. "Violla. Rellie!" Rhode shouted again.

The two mountain people broke free from the spell of the witch's gaze and ran outside. From the back of Rellie's old rattletrap, they unloaded three wooden crosses Jake Bell had given them. Bell family legend said that the rugged wooden crosses had been carved by Jake's great-great-grandfather, John Bell, and handed down generation to generation. Though the crosses had failed to destroy the witch more than a century ago, Jake and Rhode hoped they would work now.

Rellie and Violla placed two of the crosses in the church's side windows. With considerable expenditure of courage, against the still-raging winds, Rellie and Violla forced open the front door and jammed the third cross into the hinges so it wouldn't close.

Rhode shouted, "Get those children out of here now!" She continued her incantation of scripture, keeping the Bell Witch at bay, but her words seemed to make the swirling winds pick up speed and to antagonize the attacking bats, causing them to slash at Rhode more furiously.

"I'm staying here with my Dad," Mary Jane screamed. Seth and Andrew did not have to be persuaded—they made a mad dash out the door. Jake grabbed his beloved daughter Mary Jane around the waist. With a mighty struggle against the evil wind, Jake managed to get outside the church.

Rhode stood her ground. Her long white blood-stained hair flapped furiously in the twisting, swirling winds. The entire building was shaking on its foundation. She looked behind her at Rellie and Violla. They were shielding their eyes from the stare of the witch. "Remember our plan!" Rhode shouted above the howling wind.

"We won't leave you here alone!" Violla yelled.

"You must!" Rhode exclaimed, and pointed them to the door. Violla and Rellie looked at each other and nodded. They knew they had to go about their business, no matter the outcome.

As the two struggled against the wind toward the door, Rhode shouted, "Remember, you fight fire with fire!"

"No, you don't," Kate howled in anguish. She gathered her powers and tried to slam the doors shut, but the power of Rhode's scripture and the John Bell's old wooden cross prevented her.

Outside, Violla and Rellie made a mad dash to the back of Rellie's truck. "Help us!" they screamed at Jake Bell. Jake and the children had sheltered under a giant gnarled oak fifty feet away from the shaking church.

The three grabbed cans of kerosene from the old Model T and staggered back up the slight hill to the church. "Rhode said to soak the whole thing with kerosene," Rellie shouted above the raging winds.

Jake Bell looked first to Rellie and then to Violla. "You're going to burn it down!" he said incredulously. Rellie and Violla both nodded.

"Rhode said to set the whole kit and caboodle on fire!" Violla said.

"With her still in there?" Jake couldn't believe what he was hearing. He was horrified.

"That's what she said!" Violla confirmed.

Jake watched the witch through the half-open door. He remembered how the Bell Witch had killed his great-great-grandfather, John Bell, in cold blood. Then he understood. This noble woman Rhode was sacrificing herself to rid the world of this evil. He could see Rhode, steadfastly reciting her scriptures, holding the witch at bay despite the howling wind and the tormenting bats.

"Getting it done then is our victory!" Jake yelled above the maelstrom.

Jake, Rellie and Violla circled the church with the heavy canisters, making sure to soak the entire perimeter of the rickety old wood building. It was literally a firetrap now. Rellie, Jake, and Violla shook the last drops of fuel from the metal cans and tossed them into the church. The three looked at each other, now resolved to do their duty. "This is what Rhode wants!" Violla shouted. "All right," Jake said. He lit a match, shielding it from the winds. It sparked and then burned bright. The flickering flame illuminated the trio's determined faces. Jake tossed the match into the church, and slammed the door shut. The kerosene practically exploded. Within seconds the walls of the Old Glory Holiness Church were engulfed in flames.

Inside, Rhode held her ground. She continued to press forward with her recitation of the Holy Word, her right hand held high, blood trickling from dozens of cuts. The witch had been reduced to half of her normal size, but the winds that circled around her had increased speed. As the witch diminished, it seemed the winds and the winged attackers swirled faster and faster in a tight vortex. Still more bats poured in until the interior of the old church was almost black with their number.

The witch, who thought herself invulnerable, cried out when she saw the church was on fire. Kate knew that she was trapped by Rhode's powerful rendering of the Bible and the crosses guarding all the exits. There was no escape for the evil one, despite her vast powers. The flames crept higher up the walls, soon leaping to the tinder box roof. Kate whirled around, desperately seeking any way of escape. Onward and upward the fire roared, embracing up the walls with a red and orange fury. Soon the night sky was lashed by frantic, flashing flames and a rain of white ashes. The flames roared as the old timbers of the church exploded from the heat.

Steadfast Rhode never wavered from her task, not failing once in her recitation, her eyes not moving from the witch's evil glare. She didn't falter even though she was drenched in her own blood. Rhode was determined that she keep the witch at bay, this time for eternity. For the first time in her ancient existence, the Bell Witch was afraid. Kate the evil one now was facing a nemesis that she had not encountered before, knowledgeable and pure.

Not once did Rhode even glance at the path to safety and freedom as the flames licked up the walls and engulfed the roof. Rhode never once considered her own fate—her goal was to rid the world of this evil. It was now or never.

The greatest trick the devil and his kind, Katherine included, ever worked was to convince humankind that he and his followers do not exist. Rhode knew the truth—they existed. Her whole life was destined for this moment. She would not fail. She could not fail. Rhode knew that this meant that she was almost certain to die a horrific earthly death. Still she did not retreat.

Smoke began to swirl inside the church, mixing with the wild winds and the torrent of blood-sucking creatures. Rhode started coughing violently from the bitter, acrid smoke, but she kept speaking. The howling winds fanned the flames ever higher. The witch still had power, but true to the Gospel, Rhode's words were taking a toll. Unbelievably, the flames and heat seemed to be taking a bigger toll on Kate than the small, white-haired Rhode.

The witch began to panic, flinching in fear from the mountain woman's crystal-blue eyes. Kate spat on Rhode's uplifted right hand; her spittle was like acid, sizzling on the flesh of her palm. Still Rhode held steady. The blood around her feet began to boil from the heat that burned under the floorboards.

Outside the church, Violla, Rellie and Jake couldn't tell what was happening inside the inferno. They knew the old building, totally engulfed in flames, would collapse soon, killing their precious Rhode and ridding the world of the Bell Witch. The trio had done all they humanly could—they hoped it was enough.

The threesome reached out in the darkness of that awful night and grasped each other's hands. Those hands had been worn rough by years and years of hard mountain work; their tough upbringing gave them strength to stiffen their resolve and do what they had to do. Still Jake wondered, "Isn't there anything we can do to help Rhode?"

Now, Rellie and Violla weren't sophisticated people. They were who they were: simple mountain folk, who believed in the Good Book, the Lord, and in Rhode. They believed in the staunch woman they called sister, because they knew what type of person she was. Rhode had lived her life in a way that other people didn't. She had lived like people who go to church say they live, but don't. Rhode lived the pure and the simple life, refusing to worship money, land or worldly goods. Rellie and Violla didn't understand what brought this evil to their small Smoky Mountain village, and they didn't know exactly why Rhode had to be the one to battle this evil. This mountain couple just knew that they would do whatever was necessary to help Rhode complete her task. They had never seen anything like the Bell Witch before, never actually knew that evil like this existed. All Rellie and Violla knew was that if Rhode said she needed to destroy this creature, it was for a righteous reason. No matter how simple they may seem to the outside world, Rellie and Violla were smart in their own simple way. And the mountain couple was determined to do whatever it took to get their friend and family member through this matter. Because no matter what Rhode had told Jake, Rellie and Violla considered Rhode family. They knew she thought of them as family as well. It hurt them to leave her in a flaming crucible while trying to rid the world of a she-devil. But they understood why.

A resounding crash signaled the end of the battle. It came so abruptly, it seemed as if the whole episode had never occurred. The roof collapsed in on Rhode and the witch so violently that it created a vacuum effect and snuffed the flames out almost immediately. All that was left was a gigantic jumble of glowing embers and twisted timbers. The chimney had collapsed, but the bottom half remained. The heat had shaped the brickwork into a cross.

CHAPTER **19**

RELLIE, VIOLLA, AND Jake ran to the edge of the recent inferno, frantically searching for any sign of life. Alas, to their everlasting horror, there was none. A great sadness engulfed them all. There was no way any human being could have survived such heat, such total devastation. Could the Bell Witch have survived? They hoped not. But who knew for sure? What could any human being truly know about such an evil being that had no flesh, no bone and no soul? All they knew was that their beloved Rhode died trying with all of her courage and soul to destroy Kate, the Bell Witch. Only time would tell if the white-haired mountain woman had rid the world of this evil. Certainly Jake Bell or his daughter, Mary Jane Bell, would know—if this insidious being began to torture them again. Perhaps their descendants would find out, decades after the deaths of Jake and Mary Jane, when they became ensnared in another grisly haunting. Only then would the exact outcome of this epic battle between good and evil be known for sure.

Jake walked over to the gnarled old oak, where Mary Jane, Seth and Andrew huddled. Scared and frightened, they were none the worse for wear. They looked white as young ghosts as Jake approached them. The giant fire had spewed ash into the air and scattered it all over like a volcano. The white residue covered everything for acres, including the three children.

Jake Bell had to laugh as he approached the cinder-covered youths. "What's so funny?" Mary Jane spat out as she tried to shake ash from her long blonde hair.

Rellie and Violla stood at the foundation of the fallen church. The embers continued to snap and pop, keeping them out of the interior where they might find the remains of Rhode. Standing there, the couple reached for each other's hand, the first time they had done that in years. Hand in hand, they surveyed the area for the last time. The couple soon decided that there was little chance anyone could survive this fiery fiasco. Not even if that person was as good and close to the Lord as Rhode was.

"Come on," Jake said as he put his arms around Rellie and Violla. "Let's go home; there's nothing else to do here."

At first, Rellie and Violla were reluctant to move. "Look at that," Rellie said in wonder. "See how the chimney is collapsed into the shape of the cross?"

Jake smiled and clasped his arm tighter around Rellie. "Rellie, that is a good sign, isn't it? It's beautiful," Jake continued. He allowed the couple a few more seconds, then again urged them to leave. "You've done all you could do. Let's go home," he said.

This time, Violla and Rellie did turn from the burnt area, and reluctantly headed toward Rellie's old Model T. But all the while, they looked back over their shoulders at the smoldering ruins.

Seth, Andrew and Mary Jane ran to the old Model T, piling in the back near where the old barrel was lashed to the frame. Sadly, Rellie, Violla and Jake climbed into the black cab. They had to brush burnt ash from the interior. Rellie's vehicle was not spared from the fire's wrath.

On the third try, Rellie was able to start the Model T, and slowly but surely, the car sputtered back toward their mountain village. Not one word was spoken by anyone on the way back. It wasn't until they dropped off Seth and Andrew that anyone spoke. Jake Bell jumped out of the car and brushed the boys off. He knew that both Seth's and Andrew's parents would want to know what had happened that night. They knew that their boys were going to some kind of learning session, but now they would have lots of questions about why their boys came home covered with soot.

Jake cleared his voice and said, "Young men, we don't want to lie to your parents, but let's not upset them with the whole story of tonight's happenings until we find out . . . " Jake searched for his next few words and then said, ". . . exactly what did happen tonight. All right?"

"Yes, sir, Mr. Bell," Seth and Andrew agreed. Then Jake Bell walked the two boys up to Andrew's home, where both boys were staying that night.

The three in the truck strained to hear what Jake was saying to the parents, but could not make it out. Before long, Jake came walking back to the Model T. He opened the cranky door, made sure that Mary Jane joined him up front, and then said, "Let's go home."

Slowly but surely Rellie made the drive to the Bells's house. When they arrived, they sat for a moment in strained silence. Rellie and Violla stared straight ahead.

Jake could feel their guilt. What could he say that would make them feel better? Rhode had given her life for a cause that was . . . well, Jake didn't know how to guess how great the cause was that Rhode had sacrificed her life for. He knew that Rhode had helped him and Mary Jane, as well as the generations of Bell family members to come.

Finally, at a loss for words, Jake looked at the old couple.

"Rellie, will you come by and pick me up in the morning?"

"Sure will, Jake," was all that Rellie said, never looking at him. Violla didn't say anything; she simply stared into the deep blackness of the Smoky Mountain evening that stretched forever in front of her.

Jake took Mary Jane by the hand and stood by the truck. He couldn't think of anything to say except, "Good evening, then." He led Mary Jane away. As Jake opened the door to their home, the old Model T went creeping out of the driveway. He was sure he could hear Violla sobbing.

Jake and Mary Jane settled in to their cozy mountain home, lighting some candles and a lantern. Mary Jane looked up at her father with weary eyes and a soot-stained face.

"What did happen tonight?" the exhausted girl asked.

Jake shook his head and said sadly, "Mary Jane, I just don't know." They didn't say another word that evening. Exhaustion soon overcame both of them and they fell into a deep sleep as soon as they lay down to rest.

The sun had barely begun to peek above Mount LeConte, towering behind the Bell's home, when Jake was awakened from his fitful sleep by the growling rumble of Rellie's Model T. Jake went out the front door to meet Rellie, so he did not wake Mary Jane.

"Let's go," Rellie said bluntly, and Jake slipped into the seat beside him.

On the way back to the burned church, Jake finally gathered the courage to ask Rellie, "Do you think Rhode could have survived some way?"

"Nope," Rellie said blandly. "Don't think she would have, even if she could have. That woman had a job to do, Jake." Rellie said matter-of-factly, then spat a large wad of tobacco onto the rusting floor of the Model T.

Jake didn't have anything else to say. He and Rellie never said another word.

When they arrived, Rellie pulled right up to the still-smoldering rubble. The sickening smell of burnt wood permeated the air, drowning out the sweeter fragrances of the Smoky Mountains.

The remnants of the building had cooled enough that Rellie and Jake could walk through the remains of the church house. Kicking at the scorched timbers, they looked for something, anything, that could help them resolve the question of Rhode's death.

Jake Bell was looking for some answers. Was Kate, the Bell Witch, really dead? Or was she just gone for a few years, only to return and torture his family again? The two silent men crisscrossed the burnt-out foundation. Occasionally they kicked up a red-hot ember, but for the most part, the entire area had settled into a slow smoldering ruin. There was no sign of the thousands of bats that had tortured Rhode the night before.

"I see the chimney collapsed," Jake noted, as he kicked at the bricks.

"Yup," Rellie replied, not looking up. The chimney, which had magically taken the form of a cross the previous evening, had collapsed into just a pile of red bricks.

Neither of the men knew exactly what they were looking for. From what Jake had seen the previous night, he expected to find a macabre scene. The bones or some other sign of the departed Rhode. But neither he nor Rellie could find any remnants of the terrifying confrontation that had occurred the previous evening.

"Look at this!" Rellie suddenly exclaimed. The old mountain man reached down and picked something out of a tangle of smoking timbers.

"What is it?" Jake asked. Rellie slapped a few embers away, and then held up a small article for Jake to see.

"It's a pin!" Rellie shouted. Jake strained to see. True enough, it was an old-fashioned pin that women had used for years for decoration, for placement in hats or when sewing. But where it should have been scorched or melted, instead it was shiny as a new penny. "I'll be dadburned," Rellie declared.

Jake muttered to himself, so low so that his mountain buddy could not hear him. "Yeah, I'll be dadburned, too," Jake sighed. He called out, "Rellie, I've seen that before." Jake cursed silently to himself. He had not really seen that specific item before—Jake Bell recognized the item as part of the Bell family legend.

Jake had finally seen enough. He turned away from the burned church and trudged back to the Model T. His slumped shoulders told all of his story. There probably would not be any signs of Rhode, but Jake felt sure that neither he nor his family had heard the last of the Bell Witch.

"Hey Jake, look at this!" Rellie yelled at his back.

"I'm going, Rellie," Jake said, not looking back as he reached for the door of the old black Model T.

"Jake Bell, look at this!" Rellie demanded, and this time there was something in his voice that caught Jake's attention. Jake turned around to see what Rellie had dangling from his hand.

"It's a cross, Jake. It's the cross that Rhode wore around her neck all the time. She never took it off. An old Parish priest in New Orleans gave it to her when she was studying down there. Rhode got sick with some kind of fever, yellow fever, swamp fever or something. Anyway, Jake, the old priest nursed her back to health and gave her this little gold cross." Rellie held the sparkling cross high over his head for Jake to see.

"Rhode always said that the old priest and this little cross had gotten her life back. Rhode told Violla and me she would never take it off again as long as she lived." Rellie held the small cross down at eye level to view the treasured relic more clearly. "As far as I know," Rellie said, surveying its simple beauty, "it looks like she never did."

"Well, I will be dadburned," Jake muttered again under his breath, this time with a huge sigh of exhilaration. Jake had noticed Rhode's plain gold cross the night she brought Mary Jane back to the house after the bat had bitten her. Jake had noticed the cross only because it had slipped out from around Rhode's neck as she tended to his daughter's wound. In his mind's eye, Jake remembered how the delicate cross dangled only momentarily, glistening as it reflected the light of the fire. Now Jake felt that it was meant for him to see Rhode's cross. There was no way it could have survived the inferno of the night before. It should have melted into the ash of the wreckage. But the precocious cross had survived!

Maybe the Bell family hadn't heard the last of the Bell Witch. But this simple gold cross, which had survived in the red-hot crucible that was the battle of good versus evil, gave him such a jolt of faith that Jake actually smiled. Then Jake realized something. It was the first time he had smiled in a long, long time.

EPILOGUE

Adams, Tennessee
Present Day

IT WAS A beautiful, sky-high summer day in Adams, Tennessee. A delightful young family checked out what they believed to be the real estate deal of the decade. The mother, father and young daughter walked around an ivy-covered, dilapidated home on the outskirts of Adams.

The trio managed to walk through the weed-choked yard and approach the abandoned old home.

"I know it doesn't look like much, but the contractors say that in six months, it will look like new," the young father excitedly explained as the family climbed up onto the porch.

"Ouch!" the youngster yelled out in pain.

"What happened?" the mother asked.

"I stepped on something, Mother, and it cut my foot." The daughter grimaced as she pulled an old-time stick pin from the bottom of her foot.

"Darling girl, I told you no good could ever come from walking around with no shoes on."

"Sorry, Mother," the daughter said, as she rubbed the bottom of her foot. She hid the pin in her pocket.

"Come on guys; let me show you the house," the father said as he tried to pull a board off one of the windows.

"Katherine, our real estate agent, tells me that this will be a showplace."

Beyond the house, not visible to anyone, covered by decades of wisteria vines and kudzu, sat a rusting 1928 Ford truck with an empty Jack Daniel's bottle on the floorboard.

A single black bat fluttered and soared high overhead, in the clear blue Tennessee sky.

Amen.

BELL WITCH
the movie

EVERY LEGEND HAS A SOUNDTRACK

EVERY LEGEND HAS A SOUNDTRACK

BELL WITCH
the movie

19 Original and Traditional Songs from BELL WITCH, The Movie

Featuring Jimbo Whaley, Valerie Smith & Liberty Pike, Becky Buller, Jeff & Vida Band, The Wells Family, The Jeanette Williams Band, & Marshal Andy Smalls

Jimbo Whaley

Valerie Smith & Liberty pike

With Special Guests

Betsy Palmer

Marshal Andy Smalls

Available Now From Penny Jar Records at: Target.com, Borders.com, Waldenbooks.com, VirginMega.com, Tower.com, CDBaby.com, CDNow.com, iTunes Music Store, & Amazon.com

Welcome to Adams, TN a sleepy little town whose history is a nightmare.

Walk through haunted fields with specter dogs and pay your respects at John Bell's grave. His cause of death? The Bell Witch. She calls herself "Kate." Even the State of Tennessee recognizes that she alone was the demise of John Bell in 1820, and the source of the Bell family's torment for years - perhaps even to this day. Hosted by Dr. Larry Clifton, The Official Bell Witch Video guides you through Adams with actual footage and reenactments of documented events to tell you the true story behind the legend and give you a glimpse into the past terror that was the Bell Witch.
Watch it - if you dare.

Available on DVD today at www.bellwitchvideo.com

Note: This product is not BELL WTCH: The Movie and is an advertisement for a Bell Witch Documentary

Robert Maughon, M.D.

Author
of
BELL WITCH: The Movie NOVEL

Robert Mickey Maughon, M.D. is a graduate of the University of Tennessee and the University of Tennessee Medical School in Memphis.

Dr. Maughon trained in Internal Medicine at Tulane University in New Orleans. His other published books include *Elvis Is Alive* and *New Orleans E.R.*

Donna Maughon is a graduate of the University of Tennessee and studied four years at Tennessee's School of Architecture in Knoxville. She edits all of Dr. Maughon's novels.

S. SHANE MARR

Producer and Director of
BELL WITCH: The Movie

S. Shane Marr is a filmmaker. At age eight, he picked up his parents' Super 8 Film Camera and shot his first film, *It Came from the Toy Box*, a clay animated short film. From that day forward, all Shane ever wanted to do was make movies and entertain others. By age 14, Shane had his own local television talk show. He earned a diploma from The Professional Academy of Broadcasting at the age of 17.

Always an ingénue in the entertainment industry, Shane was asked to attend a one-time film school in association with Steven Spielberg at Universal Studios Florida. After graduation, he chose to remain at Universal Studios Florida, where he opened an office in the Film Complex to produce his own projects and also taught film classes at Full Sail Real World Education.

Noting that filmmaking was changing in Florida, Shane moved his company to Santa Monica, California, where he met many influential people. One day he met a technician who said something quite memorable: "With technology changing, you can be anywhere and make movies." This caused a light to go off in Shane's head. He immediately made plans to bring his company back home to Tennessee. Once there, he opened Cinemarr Entertainment. Soon a sister company, Big River Pictures, was formed for the sole purpose of making movies.

For *BELL WITCH: The Movie,* Shane brought some of the best cast and crew in the film industry together to complete the project, including two OSCAR-winning sound mixers. The film is shot in high-definition with the Sony 24p Cinealta Camera. In addition, he produced the motion picture soundtrack, which has 19 songs comprised of traditional, bluegrass, country and Americana music as well as original compositions specific to *BELL WITCH: The Movie.*

Shane has produced and directed many award-winning films and documentaries. Thus far in his career, Shane has won six FMPTA Crystal Reel Awards, eleven TELLY Awards, two AXIEM Awards, a Videographer Award of Distinction, and two Houston Worldfest Awards for Best Director.

BETSY PALMER

A Legend in Her Own Time

Betsy Palmer was a favorite face in the legendary "Golden Age of Live Television," which included her participation in "I've Got a Secret" and "The Today Show." In addition, Ms. Palmer was a distinguished Broadway performer—including *The Grand Prize* (her 1954 debut), *Same Time Next Year*, and *The Eccentricities of a Nightingale* (a reworking of *Summer and Smoke* done by Tennesee Williams) plus numerous revivals—and film actress (*Mr. Roberts* and *The Tin Star* starring Henry Fonda and John Ford's *The Long Grey Line* starring Tyrone Power).

Ms. Palmer became a famed favorite in the cult classic, *Friday the 13th*, in which she played the mad Mrs. Voorhees, the legendary mother of the psychopathic Jason. The twenty-five-year-old movie retains a huge fan base and set a standard for the adolescent-slash film.

Having always been a great fan of Betsy Palmer, S. Shane Marr, director of *BELL WITCH: The Movie*, asserted that she—and no other actress—was to be the "Voice" of the devilish Kate. Since then, Big River Pictures and Ms. Palmer have entered into a uniquely friendly collaboration.

So, *BELL WITCH: The Movie*—though set in the early nineteenth century—has given a twenty-first century honor to a preeminent performer, Ms. Betsy Palmer.

Originating the role of Kate, the Bell Witch, Ms. Palmer solidifies a legendary talent in one of the eeriest movies of our time, from one of the strangest legends in American folklore history.

Betsy Palmer signs a *BELL WITCH: The Movie* poster.

Cinemarr Entertainment and Big River Pictures are located near the Great Smoky Mountains National Park in East Tennessee.

Other novels by Robert Mickey Maughon, M.D.
NEW ORLEANS ER
ISBN: 0-9650366-0-X

ELVIS IS ALIVE
ISBN: 0-9650366-2-6
Available at all bookstores and on the Internet

For more information about *BELL WITCH: The Movie* please visit **www.bellwitchthemovie.com**

For more information about the music in *BELL WITCH: The Movie* and to purchase the CD visit **www.bellwitchmusic.com**